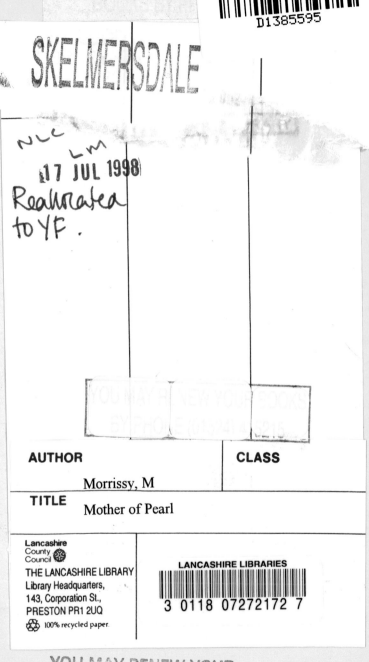

Mother of Pearl

Mary Morrissy was born in Dublin in 1957. She won the
Hennessy Award for short stories in 1984 and her stories
have appeared in several magazines, newspapers and
anthologies including *Best Short Stories 1992* and *New
Writing 2* (1993). Her first collection, *A Lazy Eye*, was
published in 1993 and has just been reissued in Vintage.
She won a Lannan Literary Award in 1995. She reviews
fiction for the *Irish Times* and the *Independent on Sunday*
and lives in Dublin.

by the same author

A LAZY EYE

Mary Morrissy

———

Mother of Pearl

JONATHAN CAPE
LONDON

07272172

First published 1996

3 5 7 9 10 8 6 4 2

© Mary Morrissy
Mary Morrissy has asserted her right
under the Copyright, Designs and Patents Act, 1988
to be identified as the author of this work

First published in the United Kingdom in 1996 by
Jonathan Cape,
Random House, 20 Vauxhall Bridge Road, London SW1V 2SA

Random House Australia (Pty) Limited
20 Alfred Street, Milsons Point, Sydney,
New South Wales 2061, Australia

Random House New Zealand Limited
18 Poland Road, Glenfield,
Auckland 10, New Zealand

Random House South Africa (Pty) Limited
PO Box 337, Bergvlei, 2012 South Africa

Random House UK Limited Reg. No. 954009

A CIP catalogue record for this book
is available from the British Library

Papers used by Random House UK Limited are natural,
recyclable products made from wood grown in sustainable forests.
The manufacturing processes conform to the environmental
regulations of the country of origin.

ISBN 0–224–04037–5

Printed and bound in Great Britain by
Mackays of Chatham PLC

For my mother

Acknowledgments

I am indebted to Dr Noël Browne's autobiography *Against the Tide* for an overview of the TB epidemic in Ireland and John Molloy's *Alive Alive O* courtesy of the Gilbert Library, Dublin and Irish Collection, for his first-hand account of daily life in sanatoria.

Special thanks also to Sinéad Matine, Marych O'Sullivan, Joanne Carroll, John Vincent, Séamus Martin and Joan Forde and grazie to Paul Cahill and Fernando Trilli. For all her work, my agent, Carol Heaton, to the Arts Council of Ireland for a literature bursary which aided in the writing of this book and to the *Irish Times* for that most precious of commodities – time.

PART ONE

IT HAD STARTED as a shadow on Irene Rivers' lung. She was eighteen, the new cashier at The Confectioner's Hall (she was quick with figures). Autumn was in the air. Russet and gold. A playful breeze leapt out cheekily at the street corners; the silver-backed waves cavorted as if in the last hour of play before dark. The *Queen Bea* was making its way into the harbour, the blue stripe on its funnel like a festive ribbon as if the liner were a huge, floating gift. It glided, a colossus, between the huddled houses. Crowds of passengers lined the decks, shielding their eyes against the defiant sun and waved – poignantly – as Irene turned away from the sea.

The interior of the hospital was umber, dolorous as a church, the equipment mounted on a platform, a tabernacle housing an all-seeing eye. Irene felt the cold photographic plates press against her chest, heard the radiographer bark – chin up, deep breath, hold – and feared the worst. She didn't have to see the clouded blue picture of her lungs, the flowery clumps of infection. From the moment she surrendered to the embrace of a device that rendered her transparent, there was a shadow not only on Irene's lung, but on her life too.

Granitefield. Superstitiously, no one called it the sanatorium though in the end the mere mention of the name Granitefield was enough to signal death and the illness that

3

dared not be spoken of. Irene was acclaimed there, the one the nurses pointed to as proof of cure. *Our* Irene, they called her, when no one else did. Her mother, horrified by the notion that she might have contaminated the family (though, in fact, the opposite was the case; years of living in a damp, quayside house had aggravated Irene's condition), would have nothing more to do with her. She had, by her illness, disgraced the household, her mother believed. It spoke of poverty, a lack of hygiene. Her brothers dared not visit her. They would have had to explain their absence to a mother obsessed with contagion. Instead they helped to scour her room and burn her bedding. What they remembered of her shamed them. The skirmishing in the kitchen on the last day of their father's shore leave almost two decades before. A lighthouse keeper, he lived on a cathedral of rock, a prisoner of the elements. Stroked only by an incessant beam and the beating of the waves against his citadel, his horizon determined by the mood of the furious sea. He was a stranger to his own, a brooding, silent man. Porter made him morose but it was people who demented him. After months of solitude, the rowdy pubs, the thronged seafront, their cramped and dingy house seemed to torment him. In the midst of this human surfeit the waves would suddenly roar in his head, the vicious dazzle of the giant lantern he tended would blind him momentarily and a boiling spume would swell within him; he lashed out at whoever was at hand. Jack had tried to intervene that day but what he came upon so shocked him – his mother straddled on the kitchen table, a great marbled breast exposed, her skirts rumpled around a shady crotch, his father rooting at her – that he turned and fled. Sonny cowered in the back yard peering through the scullery window in greedy awe at the two dim figures flailing among the shard and egg yolks. So *that* was what they did. It was the last time either son would abandon his mother.

For Irene, her father would always be the hermit in the tower on the craggy rock they called the Spaniard where he spent over half his life. She thought of him out at the edge of the land, proud and fierce, atop his beacon of light, the one fixed point in a turbulent sea. As storms lashed the coast, Irene could hear from the upstairs room on Mariner's Quay the vast bellow of foghorns in the night. Their echoes stayed with Irene and grew into a lifelong dread of lonely places. Lying between icy sheets, the winds thundering at the gable, she imagined her father out there, a wounded beast howling at the water's edge, and a fearful pity for him would seize her. It reached out across the sheltered harbour, weaving gingerly around the jagged inlets of the treacherous coastline, over the oyster-coloured mountains and finally took wing across the bilious sea. But it was a delicate connection, Irene knew, full of a feline wistfulness that could not survive in his invincible presence. The imminence of his arrival in their house – the very bricks seemed to shrink from him – was like the threat of a thunderous Force Ten. To his infant sons William Rivers loomed, much like the tower he had come from, so no matter how far they stretched back their necks they could see no end to him. And as they grew, this monumental awe he inspired turned into a treacherous respect. They circled around him, making glancing land-falls and dodging his flinty gaze.

Ellen Rivers, calcified by her husband's tidal rages and the harshness of her solitary life, served him with surly resignation. She said little, surrendering instead to the venomous interior life that fuelled her. She had hailed from a village further up the estuary now totally aban-doned. Famine and emigration had robbed it of its people; Ellen's family had been the last to leave. Like Lot's wife she had looked back on that day and had seen a crumbling jetty and a ramshackle collection of empty houses, some no more than crooked gables already sinking into the bog, and cursed the folly of loyalty and the uselessness of love.

Only Irene was spared her father's ire. He was no kinder to her than the others but he had never lifted his hand to her; in the Rivers' household this was a significant indulgence.

Her condition deteriorated during one of the stormiest winters the country had ever endured. She was sent to Granitefield in late November; her father, trapped on his rock, did not come ashore until early in the new year. He was told simply that circumstances had forced her departure. She had had to 'go away'. It implied an unwanted child.

'How else could she be?' Irene's mother told him with some relish. '*Your* daughter.'

The bus was a beast driven. It bucked and swayed. Wipers clung gamely to its snout. Inside, nervous suitcases rattled overhead. Moisture rolled down Irene's shoulder. Granitefield stood in a stretch of grizzled countryside, seeping grey stone (hence its name) giving way to barred, teeth-like windows. A few trees rose suppliant from the duncoloured fields. The hills were like bruises.

'Hold your breaths, lads, it's catching!' a passenger muttered as they shuddered to a halt at the gates. That was as close as they dared go. As Irene alighted she was aware of faces, grim and curious, pressed up against the muddied windows. She had come to accept the sleeplessness, the fevers, the bone-weary torpor, but she could not bear the leprous gaze of those who had already given her up for dead. The bus slewed around, listing as it did into a large, mud-coloured puddle, drenching her from head to foot. She felt she had been spat at. A cough rattled in her chest. It pained her. She tried to draw a breath but the louring sky would not yield up to her the portion of air that was rightfully hers. She could feel her mouth filling up. She raised a handkerchief to her lips. It came away

6

scarlet. I will die here, she thought, drowned in my own blood.

They put her in a bathing hut. A white pavilion, intricate of eave. It is high summer already; time has flown. She is the child kept in from play. Outside a blue tumult. She can hear the thud of footsteps on the boardwalk. Somewhere a tiny band is playing, or is it the blurred wheeze of an organ-grinder? There is the whip and flap of bunting, the high shrieks of bathers. A skinny boy, showing off, leaps from the jetty, arms outstretched, head thrown back, his legs cycling wildly in the air. Irene strains to hear the jubilant splash but it never comes. Instead the door of the white room opens and it is she who is in the water, adrift on a sea of pain, great, glinting waves of it that shatter into thousands of tiny shards before her eyes. The liner is going down, rent in two. She is huddled in the bow of a lifeboat, a shivering survivor. Icebergs, white and enormous as the pain, groan and creak, jostling to crush the damp timbers of her life raft. There is a ferocious snap as the mountains of ice, now open-jawed sharks, gnaw their way through the sea-rotten ribs that hold her little boat together. The timbers gape. She is swallowed by the deep . . .

The operation, they told her, had saved her. But she had lost four of her ribs, cracked open by a giant pair of shears. The pleural fluid which had clogged in her chest had been dispersed but Irene felt a dizzying vacuum where the congestion had been. The knowing gaze of the X-ray, trawling through the blue seabed of her innards, had been followed by the hands of a surgeon who had made a forced entry, kneading the soft, red, pulpy heart of her. Without her ribs Irene felt as if part of her protection against the world had been removed. It was not only the mutilation but the fact that her bodily home had been tampered with, a gable wall torn away and like a half-demolished house, the colour of the chimney breast, the trimmings of the parlour exposed to all.

As a patient, Irene learned to kill time. She acquired the prisoner's knack of being able to drop off to sleep at any time. Whole days could be drowsed away that way, the long, grey afternoons in particular, which yawned and stalled, tickingly silent after the clamour of the mornings. They were woken in the eggshell dawn with a swish of curtain, a pumping of pillows, the rattle of breakfast trolleys. A mess of yolk, a slice of thinly toasted bread already curling at the edges, were slapped down on their trays.

'Tea!' Bridget from the kitchens would yell like the last call of the stationmaster.

'Medication!'

These were the destinations of their day.

The cleaners came in at eight to buff the floors, the clattery din of their buckets and mops like the tattoo of an advancing army. They moved swiftly through the wards working stealthily under the beds and into unused corners. It seemed to Irene like a punishment, this daily scouring, as if they were suspected of having smuggled in germs overnight. Invisible to the invaders, the patients lay trapped in their beds – stranded on high ground – while beneath them the very floor they walked on was purged. If she had set her leg down, Irene was con- vinced that it too would have got the blind blessing of a cloth.

And then, the doctors . . . .

Later, out of isolation, wrapped up and pushed out on the verandah to take the air, Irene learned to play cards. Beggar My Neighbour, Fish in the Pond, Old Maid, as if they were rain-bound children at the seaside. Her neighbour in the next bed was a nun, Sister Baptist. She dealt decorously, holding her cards close to her chest.

'Now, poker, I'd be game for that,' Charlie Piper would say, 'a bit of honest-to-God gambling.'

Charlie Piper. These names would haunt Irene. Charlie Piper sold fire extinguishers. Selling and quelling, he used to say, that's my game. Charlie Piper tried to escape by rowing across the lake. He thought he could cheat death by a simple act of daring. It was a frosty night. He pushed off from the rotting jetty and rowed out, plashing softly across the still surface. But there were currents out there and he hadn't the strength to row back. They found him slumped in the boat which had got tangled in reeds near the far shore. He had almost made it to the other side.

'That's not the spirit, Mr Piper,' Sister Baptist would reply tartly. 'We play for the fun of it.'

Despite the lack of gain, Sister Baptist played with an exacting energy.

'Snap!' she would cry, gleefully gathering up a winning bundle. The games brought out the savage in her. Victory made her wilful and greedy.

Mr Powers peered over his spectacles, his jowls quivering. He had been a schoolmaster, though in Granitefield, Irene realised, it did not much matter what you had once been. She could imagine Mr Powers, a once portly man whose flesh was caving in now, stalking between the schoolboy rows rapping on the desks with his cane or bawling out the roll call. He would know his pupils only by their surnames. When he wasn't pacing in the aisles he would stand at the back of the class so they would not know where he was at any given moment. And he would wait for the first boy to peer back over his shoulder . . .

But they had exacted their revenge. While he had been hearing tables, his charges had infected him.

At cards he was never quite quick enough. He pouted when he missed but played on manfully, confident now only of defeat.

'Pick one from the top,' Sister Baptist would bark at him.

He was bullied into death, slinking off before the game was finished.

Netta Cavendish grew petulant and quarrelsome at the card table. Netta blamed her dancing days for her present condition. Dance hall sawdust had irritated her breathing tubes, she said. That and a drenching after cycling home in the small hours of the morning. Like every patient at Granitefield, Netta had to justify her illness; none of them, Irene noticed, could accept the random hand of fate. It was all due to something they had done, or something they had failed to do.

'You only dealt me six,' Netta would wail.

She dithered endlessly before abandoning a card, fingering one and then another, afraid to make the final choice. She died in much the same way, refusing to relinquish because she felt she had been wronged.

The Mother of all the Boys kept the score. She was an amazon of a woman; broad in girth, her shoulders larded from farm work, her hands like hams. She wore working men's boots with the laces undone. It was almost impossible to imagine such a bulky frame surrendering to any kind of illness, and yet watching one of her coughing fits was like seeing an oak tree, huge and terrible, creaking perilously in a storm. Irene never knew her name.

'I am the Mother of all the Boys,' she would declare, 'Pascal, Mikey, Florence, Bill and little Tom.'

But they never appeared, the five strong lads she boasted of, not even when she died, crashing heavily into darkness.

Meanwhile, Sister Baptist played on. Only Irene, tenacious for its own sake, could match her.

Granitefield had been a poorhouse in famine times; the high walls remained; the blue lime-washed corridors; in one of the outhouses was the huge, cast-iron cauldron in which the communal gruel had been stewed. Everything there was named twice, like signposts in a lost native language. The isolation units – their official name – were known by the inmates as The Camp. Home to the infectious, who remained nameless, shut away, until they were pushed, blinking, into the sunlight. Thence to The Manor – as it was grandly called by the staff – the stone building visible from the road. For the ill these were The Wards. The sloping grounds which led down to the lake were referred to as The Yard. So called because every morning, the grass still wizened with hoarfrost, a duty nurse, or sometimes Matron herself, would lead snakes of patients out there for their daily constitutional. The exercise was good for them, the bracing air would revitalise their ailing lungs and punctured chests. Home to bacilli and tubercles, even their bodily parts were not their own. They were a motley bunch, their day clothes – layers of vests and woollens, greatcoats and hats – worn over regulation pyjamas. Like windswept scarecrows they tramped, two by two, down the gravel path that led to the lake shore and then, once, briskly around its perimeter. Crows cackled in the trees as they laboured, a chain-gang in search of occupation. Sometimes Irene worried that they might be led away to some strange, neglected place and abandoned. Or worse.

The route the walkers took was dotted with secret stashes – half-smoked Woodbines were hidden in the urns on the front balustrade, naggins of whiskey strapped to the underarm of the jetty – and this alone gave the daily dose of exercise the air of an excursion. There, skulking in the seeping woods among the dead leaves, a mouthful of spirits or a hurried draw of tobacco was like a draught of freedom. A taste of life.

Unfit for life they learned other skills. Afternoons in the Day Room, a crackling wireless on the go. The reception was always bad.

'Due to our position in the world,' Mr Powers said.

Which to judge from the radio was down a seething mineshaft. The sound came in waves, hissing and fading. Ernie Troubridge had taken charge of it. Ernie had been a docker; the coal dust had got him. He tinkered continuously with the radio, heaving the set about the room and perching it high up and low down, tilting it this way and that to minimise the static. He had fashioned a makeshift aerial out of a clothes hanger which stuck out like a twisted wand; it made everything much clearer, Ernie insisted. This became his occupation – carrying an angry box of sound around. Whenever he set it down he would stand over it impatiently twisting the knobs when, it seemed, the broadcasters had moved deliberately out of range. Occasionally he would thump its polished top and, scarified, it would leap to attention only to slouch again as soon as Ernie's back was turned. What pleasure he got out of listening to it Irene could never fathom. The news either irritated him or confirmed his worst suspicions, though he responded to certain items with a triumphant 'Aha!' like a poker player with a winning trick. He liked to listen to the gale warnings. 'Badweather up ahead, Cap'n,' Charlie Piper would taunt, winding his head around the door of the Day Room.

He was about his business, a thriving black market in cigarettes and oranges, a complicated moneylending scheme. Everyone owed him. Ernie Troubridge, bent in the dusk like a man in conciliatory prayer to a spitting, vengeful god, ignored the jibes.

'Tyne, Dogger, German Byte . . . falling slowly.'

And Irene Rivers would remember her lost father, keeping his lonely vigil at the edge of land, holding out against the storms.

Miniature industry flourished in the Day Room. There was Betty Long who knitted with a tight-lipped ferocity as if she were on piece-rates. She worked from two battered patterns – one a lemon-yellow matinée jacket, the other a baby-blue pair of bootees.

'Oh, Irene, look,' she would cry, fretting over lost stitches.

Irene would gently rip back to the flaw and Betty would start again. For whom the baby things were intended Irene never learned. She could have clothed an orphanage with the volume she produced but Irene suspected that she stored them away, a trousseau of candyfloss smalls for the children she would never have.

At the green baize card table Isla Forsyth did shell pictures; Babe Wrafter appliquéd; Mary Cantalow made cathedrals out of matchsticks; Sister Baptist crocheted. Small intricate things. Chalice covers, Irene guessed. Once, while showing Irene a complicated stitch, she asked sweetly, 'You are one of us, dear, aren't you?'

Irene looked at her stonily. That doughy expression, the unctuous eyes hungry for confession. She did not reply. What she believed would have shocked Sister Baptist. That there was no God; there was only sickness and health. And no one to save you but well-meaning strangers who cut you open and left a wound.

DR AUGUST CLEMENS. These were the words Irene used in prayer. Dr August Clemens. His name set him apart but he was one of *them*. A consumptive. He, too, had been cracked open like a shell, had sweated out the fevers and had been wheeled out, teeth chattering and hands blue, to inhale his icy cure. He was a stocky, robust man, his high colour the only legacy of his disease, though that seemed merely an extension of his good humour. He breezed about, coat flapping, hand perpetually raised in greeting. Ruddy-faced and foxy-haired, as if blessed with the bloom of the outdoors. The lord of the manor, some of the male patients sulkily called him, usually when he had tracked down a hideout for smokes or a gambling racket. His rude health seemed almost an offence in the midst of the ghostly sick; a defiant gesture, a fist waved in the face of God. To Dr Clemens, Irene granted the kind of loyalty which only the fiercely grateful can sustain. He was the first man to rescue her. The second would be Stanley Godwin.

'Well, my girl, good news!'

Dr Clemens sat astride a chair in his small office, his tapered beard, flecked with grey, tickling his broad forearms. In one hand, a sheaf of blue X-rays.

'All clear!'

He spoke in shorthand. Irene almost expected him to say 'over and out' at the end of his sentences.

'You can go home.'

Irene sat threading the belt of her dressing gown through her fingers. This was the moment she had been dreading. Cure. Final and irrevocable. In the six years she had been at Granitefield she had found a tranquil order, a gravity of purpose which suited her temperament. The hostile world had retreated; she could not imagine venturing out there again, orphaned and adrift.

'Well?' demanded Dr Clemens.

Irene looked beyond him. Through the grimy barred window she could see the lake shimmering. The trees, clothed for high summer, regarded her reproachfully. A mop-haired boy – she recognised him from Ward C – was trying to sail a kite by the water's edge. He threw the red triangle up in the air and made mad dashes, unwinding the string as he did from around a tin can. But there was not enough wind and each time the kite would slowly dip and sink, landing crumpled at his feet.

'Nothing to say?'

Dr Clemens looked at her with a dogged eye. She could not bear his gaze of kindliness and understanding. He understood too well; it made her uneasy. She did not wish to be so easily read.

'You don't want to go, do you?'

She shook her head miserably.

'But you're young, your whole life's ahead of you. You can put this behind you now. It's different for me, it's my life's work, you understand?'

Irene nodded; *this* she did understand. The singularity of vocation was not new to her. She had only to think of her father.

'Only a madman or a drunkard would choose to work in a place like this.' Dr Clemens gestured with his large hand (not like a surgeon's, more the weathered mitt of a sea captain) to the high, stained walls, his tilting desk propped up under one gammy leg by a large medical volume. Dust motes swam in the bath of distilled summer light. From the corridors, the crash of bedpans. 'Or an incurable . . . '

A fly buzzed around him. He swatted it away.

'Oh yes,' he said sadly, 'that's why I'm here.'

She was put to work in the kitchens with Bridget and Annie. Annie was wiry and lean-jawed with crossed eyes, which gave her a transfixed air as if some small insect had settled on the bridge of her nose. She, like Irene, had been adopted by Dr Clemens. It was a small club, Irene discovered. A nurse here, a cleaner there, had been smuggled on to the staff, a place found for them.

'We need you,' he would say to Irene referring to his secret troupe. 'We need you to fight off despair. You are on the front line.'

Bridget, on the other hand, was from the outside. She did the heavy work. Plump and able, she peeled potatoes and hoisted the large cauldrons on and off the stoves. The three of them laboured in the large, dim basement room, lighting the huge ovens and tending the gas jets which kept pots abubble all day. From early morning until darkness fell, they heaved and toiled. Irene loved the clatter and steam. After years of enforced idleness it was like finding herself suddenly on the assembly line of a munitions factory, part of the war effort. The very building seemed to sweat – the fogged windows, condensation rolling down the walls, the greasy black and red flagstones. She welcomed beads of perspiration on her own brow, no longer a sign of fever or the harbinger of confinement. She loved the kitchen's functional air, and the scale of it. The sheen of the bain-marie, the cavernous refrigerator, its door like the hatch of an aeroplane, the enamel bins marked FLOUR and SUGAR with their lean-to lids and scoops the size of shovels. The work, after what seemed a lifetime of miniature occupation, pleased her enormously. Each day a fresh start, a confirmation that life did indeed go on. The early calm gave way to a mid-morning storm, heat and panic as pots boiled over or supplies suddenly ran short. There was the clamour of dinner time, the flap and rush of bearing food in and out, the confusion, the collisions, the inevitable spillages. Then, plunging hands into sudsy water and scouring for an hour, a welcome purging. Irene's favourite time was the mid-afternoon when an eerie hush fell and they could sprawl around the scrubbed kitchen table drinking tea and picking at leftovers.

Sometimes the peace would be shattered by a request for tea in the Matron's office. It was she who often broke the bad news. Tea always helps at a time like that, Matron would say. Helped *her* at any rate, Irene would think, trying to imagine Matron (Nancy Biddulph – Irene was surprised she had a name; Charlie Piper called her the Matterhorn) tackling something as vague and enormous as death. She was more at home with the concrete indignities of the living. A smart blow on the rump after a bed bath, the quick whip of a thermometer from the rectum. She treated illness with a stiff, naval kind of jollity.

As Irene cut sandwiches and buttered scones for the bereaved, she would sometimes imagine that the guest in Matron's office was her mother, coming to claim her back now that she was cured. She would pin up her hair and take her apron off and, bearing a loaded tray through the mute corridors, she would practise her most willing and engaging smile. In Irene's version of the reunion, her mother appeared more refined and prosperous (as if she had come into money, the only circumstances Irene could imagine which would justify this new expansiveness), wearing a cloche hat and white gloves. These she would peel off, finger by gracious finger, in nervous anticipation as Irene, with an armful of shivering china, steered towards her. But the prospect was so dizzying, so delectably unbearable, that by the time Irene reached Matron's office she could only manage to knock and holler

'Tea, ma'am' before abandoning the tray outside and
fleeing.

'I used to know an Irene once,' Charlie Piper said to her
one day when she came to deliver his dinner tray. 'She was
a real goer, I can tell you! She used to . . . '

'That's quite enough, Mr Piper,' Nurse Dowd interjected, holding his thin wrist between her fingers in search
of a pulse. He was back in The Camp then; it was just after
his failed escape attempt. Irene slid the tray on to his lap.
He winked at her. His jokiness belonged to a healthy man;
here it seemed macabre.

'Ooh,' he cried in falsetto, spotting the dessert. It was a
Sunday. 'A bit of tart!'

He poked at the pale apples which fell drunkenly out
from the pastry and splayed out on to the plate, bringing
their juices with them. They were windfalls which she and
Annie had gathered in the grounds.

'Really!' Nurse Dowd scowled, and dropping his hand,
marched out. He jiggled his eyebrows at her retreating
back. He communicated by such deft arrangements of his
features, at once mocking and self-deprecating.

'Really!' he mimicked.

He spoke of women like a condemned man. Of Gloria, the
telephonist who sat in a box inside the main hall. He lusted
after her, her fat glossy lips, her painted hands, the beauty spot
high on her left cheek. Her encasement behind glass.

They traded innuendos.

'How's your lordship?' Gloria would sing out.

'Oh, picking up, darling,' he would reply, 'all the better
for seeing you.'

And then, inexplicably, he changed. One evening when
Irene came to collect his tray, he leapt out at her from
behind the door.

'Aha!' he cried. 'Gave you a fright, did I?'

He pushed the door closed and wedged a chair under the handle.

'Now, I have you!'

Irene felt a quick pang of alarm. But it was only Charlie Piper.

'Irene,' he whispered, tracing a path with his fingertips along her cheek. There was a hungry look in his eye. 'Irene . . .'

He crushed her to him, nuzzling his chin into the crook of her neck, his fingers clutching at the hair around her nape. A strange warmth invaded her limbs. It stopped her from crying out. This was just a game, she told herself. Soon he would laugh out loud and smirk at her. She felt his tongue in her ear. His hand was clutching the fabric at her breast. Playfully she tried to push him off but he had the wiry resistance of the chronically unwell. He plunged a hand beneath her blouse; a button popped. 'It's been so long,' he breathed, '*Please.*'

Over her shoulder she could see the tea tray she had left earlier, the food untouched. She fixed on it as Charlie Piper's other hand scrabbled at her crotch. He steered her towards the bed, locked in a stiff embrace. And then, suddenly, he released her. He sank on the side of the bed as if all his strength had seeped away. He held both of her hands in his.

'I just want to look.'

Mutely she complied. Unbuttoning first her tunic and peeling it away from her shoulders, then the waistband of her skirt which slid away, ballooning at her feet. She carefully undid her already molested blouse noticing the gaping buttonhole which Charlie had torn. The silky chattering of her slip up around her ears. Her vest next, of which she was ashamed. Grey and ragged-ended from too many washings; there was a rip in it now below the underarm. She unhooked her stockings and rolled them down to her ankles. She unclipped the stays of her corset, slowly, deliberately, taking care to unfasten each one when normally she would wriggle out of it before they were all undone. She concentrated on the ritual, stonily releasing the clips of her brassière – she fumbled a bit with this, her fingers working blindly away behind her back – then she lifted her breasts carefully out of the cups. It fell with a dejected flap. And then her knickers (bloomers, her mother always called them bloomers, she remembered). Calmly she edged them down over her thighs until they slipped, joining the frothy hem of stockings and skirt floating around her shoes. Her shoes. She had forgotten about her shoes. And all the time she kept her eyes on the tray. The beetroot, she could see, had bled into the hard-boiled egg.

Charlie Piper came in his hand, his eyes shut tight, his head thrown back, the cords of his neck clenched, a pulse in the hollow of his throat throbbing.

Neither of them spoke. She gathered up her fallen garments and retreating to a corner of the chalet, she clumsily redressed. He sat, head bowed. She skirted around the bed to fetch the tray; there were ten more to collect and she was way behind time now. There was an ashtray on the bedside locker. It was a bright canary-yellow with 'Souvenir of St Helier' in green writing around the rim. She fingered it briefly. Charlie turned around.

'Neilus Grundy,' he explained. 'Fell down on his last payment. Not that it's much use here. Or where I'm going for that matter.' His face brightened.

'You take it, go on.' He flashed a grin. 'Something to remember me by!'

CHARLIE PIPER must have told the others. The male patients used to gather after church on Sundays and talk among themselves. Talk dirty, Irene suspected. Dressed up in their shiny suits and shirts with threadbare collars (Irene was able to calculate how long a man was 'in' by the cut and fashion of his suit), they became the men they had been on the outside. They regained their stature even though their clothes had been made for bigger men. They stood in knots outside the chapel sizing up the female patients, who also dressed for the occasion. The women did not rely on the clothes they had brought in with them. Sisters would arrive on visiting days with a borrowed dress, or a pair of stilettos would be smuggled in courtesy of the bed-mechanic. If Dr Clemens thought the recreation period in the Day Room on Saturday evenings catered for his patients' social needs, he was sorely mistaken. The real exchange took place on Sunday mornings during Mass. Notes were passed, trysts arranged and a great deal of ogling went on among the pews. There was an air of suppressed gaiety which rose with their voices to the vaulted roof of the chapel. They sang lustily despite their coughs for the glory, not of God, but of health. Of survival. And afterwards they indulged their capacity for survival by flirting and gossiping, or resorting to forlorn tussling in the woods behind The Camp.

Irene had never 'paired off'. In the early years she had concentrated on getting well and getting out. She had thought it was a simple matter of picking up her life where she had left it. As if that lunch hour when she had left The Confectioner's Hall to go for the X-ray had merely been extended. She had asked Julia Todd to put a cream horn by for her and she liked to think of it sitting there in the shelf beneath the till, the cream and jam smearing the greaseproof wrapping, kept for her return, as if no time at all had passed. She was wearing her uniform when she left, a striped pinny and a white Miss Muffet hat. During her first months at Granitefield she worried that she had never returned the uniform. She feared it would militate against her getting her job back. She would wonder who was filling in for her now, and if they were getting the tots right. Every week she would check in the newspaper to see how she was doing. Each patient had a number so that relatives would know how they were faring, even if they couldn't visit. B4704: infectious. B4704: critical. B4704: fair. She wondered if Jack or Sonny ever opened these pages to seek her number out? Did they even know what it was? Or her father? She remembered how when she was small he would come up behind her and, swooping from behind, would toss her high in the air, crying 'And how's my little girl?' Or he would nuzzle his head in the crook of her neck and make growling sounds. Why, she wondered, did he care no longer? What punishment was this, and when would she be forgiven? She worried away at these questions but to no avail. And as the months went by and nobody from home or work materialised at Granitefield, it slowly dawned on Irene that she would never go back to *that* life. It was going on, but without her.

It was Arthur Baxter who first approached her one Sunday morning, bearing a box of chocolates.

'These,' he said, 'are for you.'

He was a big man with a sad, sagging face. The skin on his knuckles as he clutched the box, was stretched and sheeny but it hung from his face in pendulous folds like an ill-fitting coat.

'Why, thank you, Arthur . . .'

A gift, particularly in Granitefield, was as rare and wondrous as a smile from a beloved.

'I thought you might be able to help me,' Arthur said, still holding the chocolates hostage.

'Oh?' Irene said. 'In what way?'

He looked at her queasily. 'Charlie Piper says that you might be able to render me a service . . .'

It was always done in darkness. In the boiler room at the back of the camp, or the spit room where they boiled the sputum, or the mortuary. As she stripped, Irene would think of the many times she had done this for Dr Clemens, how he had poked and prodded, listening intently to the workings of her congested chest and clogged lungs. He did not seem to see the exterior, her breasts, her bare shoulders, goose-pimples rising on her forearms. No, he saw only a collection of livid organs, the pictures of which she had seen so often that she began to recognise herself only by them. She feared that one day she would look in the mirror and see a blue skeleton, a trellis of ribs and two pear-shaped sacs that were her lungs. To be watched as she undressed had been robbed of any erotic allure; she felt she was revealing very little. She had already been seen through, down to the marrow of her bones.

They were invariably grateful, the infectious ones. Shut up in their little coops all day, their arms picked up and dropped for pulse-taking, their mouths a receptacle for thermometers, their chests and backsides like pin cushions, they longed for a touch that lingered. Someone to pause, hand on flesh, to marvel at this breast bone, that hollowed-out nape, the wing of an eyebrow, to stroke the shattered line of a ribcage or the ghostly shadow of a haunch. She had her rules. She would never let them penetrate her. If they wanted gratification they must do it themselves. She could touch them, but they must never lay a finger on her. Irene would remain a virgin; she was saving herself. *This* was her calling, she believed, her life's work.

At first the names had faces. Billy Ratchett; Mossie Watling; Matthew Bennett. Matthew gave her nylons, Mossie traded with scented soap. Billy Ratchett had unwittingly left her a calendar stalled at the month of his death. It showed a Swiss chalet, its wooden gable set against an apron of blue.

'The great sanatorium in the sky,' he had said, laughing grimly. Phil Morgan, John Conway, Jim Thorpe . . . afterwards they became blurred, a procession of the wounded, whom Irene recalled with the helpless fondess of a mother for her absent, roving sons.

Davy Bly worked in the laundry. It was a place of torture for clothes. Pyjamas, bed linen and towels emerged from it thin and scratchy as if they, too, had caught a debilitating, terminal disease. The battering they got seemed like a mirror of the nerve-racking round of injections and rib-cracking their owners endured. Davy, another of Dr Clemens' refugees, fed the stolid machines which laboured constantly, drumming away softly against one another. They looked as if they were being put through some kind of drill as they harrumphed into action and shuddered together in a comradely fashion. The high tide of suds rising in their portholes and the constant thrum made the laundry feel like an infernal cabin deep in the bowels of a ship, close to the engine room. Irene had never liked Davy. She distrusted his goitred eye, his drinker's face. She found his bulbous gaze and the spittle which gathered in the corners of his mouth lewd. And she had seen him handle things, the innards of the machines, for example, as if there was some secret gratification in it.

He did errands 'for the lads' as he called them, 'backing the gee-gees' or smuggling in drink. As a patient, Irene had secretly cheered such anarchy; now she saw it as a reneging of duty. Davy, another ex-patient, was on the front line; he did not take his responsibilities seriously. He cornered her one evening when she arrived to deliver a basket of soiled teatowels from the kitchens. Years of practice had made Irene alert as a wild animal to the swoopings of men's appetites. Nobody would ever surprise her as Charlie Piper had done. The moment she entered the steamy laundry she sensed his tense readiness, the gathering of limbs for ambush.

'More of your dirty washing, eh?' he said with an odd air of menace. He was standing lazily by one of the machines, arms folded with the satisfied air of one who has delivered an opening shot. Even the din was menacing, Irene thought. The machines seemed to thunder like the pulse of Davy's evil intent.

'Where shall I leave it?'

'Anywhere you like,' he said, smirking. 'You haven't been fussy up to now, have you?'

'What do you mean?'

'I know what you're up to, I know what you do.'

He raised a hand and for a minute she thought he was going to strike her, but it was only to point a finger.

'You go around here, Miss Holier Than Thou, looking down on the likes of me, doing favours for the lads, and if I make a few bob on the side, what harm? But you!'

He jabbed his finger at her. His hands, which she always expected to be filthy, were flakily clean.

'You're nothing but a tramp. And Charlie Piper is your pimp!' He licked his lips and smiled triumphantly.

It had never struck Irene that Charlie had been exacting a price for his referrals. Sickened, she saw how she had been duped, her life's work degraded, her crusade besmirched; they had turned her into a whore. Irene set the basket down.

'What do you want?'

'I wonder what your precious Dr Clemens would think about this . . . ' Irene shuddered. She could not bear for *him* to know. He would not understand that she had done this for him, her small equivalent of his sacrifice. He would see it as Davy did, that she had sold herself for favours.

'I'm sure we can come to some arrangement between ourselves, don't you?'

IRENE KNEW THE moment she saw Stanley Godwin that he was watching someone beloved die. Healthy people keeping vigil seemed to take on the symptoms of the disease. Fevered of eye and given to an unhealthy flush, their watchfulness made them gaunt and wasted as a patient in the last stages of consumption. Of being consumed. Irene was an expert in these things; she had spent ten years at Granitefield.

Stanley visited Granitefield twice a week; it was a long journey from the capital. His mother had come south to tend an ailing sister, but it was she who had fallen ill, and now faced death in a strange place. As in much else, Stanley blamed himself. He was a burly, tender man of forty-seven. His hair was thinning on top; soon his crown would be exposed, wrinkled and puzzled as a baby's pate. His frame, robust from a lifetime of physical work, eclipsed an innate deference: a wish to be left alone, to be let be. He spent hours with his mother, who was gone beyond conversation now (though even when she could talk, Stanley's visits were punctuated by long, amiable silences). He read passages from the Bible to her or simply sat there with the air of a man deep in prayer. But inwardly he was quaking. He could comprehend the impending loss; what he couldn't imagine was his life afterwards. A middle-aged man about to be granted unwanted freedom.

His mother had raised him alone. A father was never mentioned and Stanley grew up barely believing in him. His mother had seemed to him large and mysterious enough, like a capacious cathedral, to have produced him on her own. He never felt a void in the household, nor was he curious about a man who had never become flesh, who existed only because Stanley knew he must have. He and his mother had lived together for almost half a century, their labour neatly divided. He earned the bread. She cooked and sewed and mended invisibly. Their companionship was one of necessity and did not need to be greatly indulged. A man and his mother. He came home to the smell of clothes drying over the range, a hot meal on the table and no questions asked. They both understood the contract they had made.

Heather Godwin suspected that when Stanley was younger there might have been opportunities he had turned down – there must have been girls and once, she knew, he had had a chance to emigrate to the New World. But he had never spoken of it and she had never pried. What Stanley's mother didn't know was that the girl and the New World had been the one choice.

She had been Rose Toper. They went to the pictures together. Stanley liked the cinema, sitting up close to the screen (though Rose complained it gave her a crick in her neck) and being enveloped in the big, grainy faces and the booming soundtrack. Rose sat beside him, a proprietorial arm wrapped around his, her head on his shoulder. Stanley found this paralysing, this unsought-for closeness; it made him afraid. He felt he was being bullied – most tenderly – but bullied, none the less. Stealthily, Rose was trying to take possession. She it was who had nudged Stanley into asking her out. Left to his own devices, he would have done nothing. She worked in the post office, at the savings grill where he lodged for his mother once a week. She was a severe looking girl, a thin, bony face, framed by a clipped auburn fringe. Someone not to be trifled with, Stanley thought, as he watched her, rubber-thimbled, riffling through notes or stacking coins with her careful talons. He was wrong; Rose wished earnestly to be trifled with. Initially cautious and polite, she took to flirting with Stanley in the end to elicit a response.

'Mr Godwin!' she would declaim cheerily and a little too loudly for Stanley's liking when he approached the counter. 'My favourite customer! Always lodging, never withdrawing!'

After a while even her pleasant 'How can I help you?' became weighted with obligation for Stanley. Something, he knew, was expected. Finally, exasperated, Rose shoved a note under the grill to him. 'Meet you at the Palace. Eight o'clock show. *Lost Horizon.*'

She was twenty-nine and she wanted to be married. She had lighted on Stanley because she knew he was a good man. And he was a saver. She did not realise – and would not for some time – that Stanley already had a companion, a woman who literally meant the world to him.

At first, her brusqueness reassured Stanley. She took charge as if their weekly visits to the cinema, their Sunday afternoon walks, the day trips to the sea were part of a programme prescribed for an invalid. She talked about work. He heard all the gossip from the post office, the grievances and rivalries of her life inside the cage.

'When you sit behind the grill long enough,' she told him once, 'you begin to think it is the customers who're trapped, locked in, and you are on the outside . . . ' She laughed her big, brave laugh.

She would grab his hand roughly, or thump him merrily on the shoulder, the only way she knew it was safe to touch him. She proceeded with caution. This was the man Rose was going to marry; she had plenty of time, she reasoned. Their first kiss, seven months from the day they had first walked out together and after they had progressed from hand-holding to Rose planting his arm firmly around her waist, was a shock to Stanley. Not in itself but in the determination of Rose's embrace.

At thirty-three, Rose Toper was no closer to marriage. Their careful kisses under her tutelage, her anxiously tailored passion had failed to budge Stanley. They would go back to her digs sometimes and resort to a kind of furtive groping that reduced both of them to a state of tousled breathlessness like children engaged in energetic horseplay. But it all seemed to no avail. Rose knew, of course, about his mother, though the two women had never met. Indeed, in her darker moments, Rose wondered if she existed and toyed with the notion that Stanley had a wife and children hidden away somewhere. But she knew enough of him to know he was not capable of wilful deception, which made what she had come to see as his obduracy even more incomprehensible. He acted as if there was some insurmountable obstacle to their union.

She decided to give him one last chance. She cashed in all her savings and booked a passage for America. She had a cousin there who had done very well – her husband was a realtor (Rose did not know what this meant but was none the less impressed); they had three children and a detached, timber-frame house. Rose told Stanley all of this with pointed emphasis. Mistakenly she thought that because this was what she wanted all she had to do was to dangle it in front of him to make him want it too. But it seemed barely to register.

'Mmn, that sounds nice,' he would say absently as if such a proposition could not possibly include him.

'I'm going to go,' she warned him.

He would miss her, Stanley told her. And he would. Rose was the best friend Stanley Godwin had ever had. Her busy affection, her awkward brand of mateyness, Stanley would, and did, miss.

'Think of it,' she said, 'the Statue of Liberty!' She stood with her arm thrown up in mock imitation. '*We* could be there! The New World!'

Stanley never even considered it. It was too grand, too conspicuously foreign a notion. Rose was holding out a version of the world he did not believe existed. And in the end, she left without him, heartsore but defiant, and relentlessly hopeful. Three months later she wrote to say she was marrying a longshoreman.

Stanley and his mother simply continued on. They were not people to long after things it was not rightfully theirs to hope for. What might have been were words that did not enter into their vocabulary. She had not asked Stanley to make sacrifices on her behalf, in the same way as he had not asked her to take in laundry when he was a boy to make ends meet. For both of them these were the givens of life. Now, for Stanley, at Granitefield, one of those givens was being taken away.

'*And now two women, harlots both of them came and stood in the royal presence. Justice, my lord! said one of them. This woman and I share a single house and there, in her presence, I gave birth to a child; three days after my delivery, she too gave birth. Then, one night, she overlay her child as she slept and it died. So, rising at dead of night, when all was still, she took my son from beside me, my lord, while I slept; put him in her own bosom, and her dead son in mine. . . .*'

Irene watched Stanley Godwin with bafflement. His plangent devotion puzzled her. He was like a child in pain mutely appealing for an explanation. It wasn't that he lacked dignity. In her time at Granitefield Irene had seen extraordinary scenes of grief. Once an hysterical mother who had lost her child sobbed and screamed in The Wards for hours; she would have no one touch her; it was as if the pain had stripped her skin off. Stanley would not be like this, Irene knew. What mesmerised and appalled her was his lack of pride; all of his softnesses were on show.

Stanley had noticed Irene too. When he left his mother it was not to Dr Clemens or to Matron he entrusted her in his mind; it was to Irene. When he thought of Granitefield, as he did daily, it was Irene he thought of. She became for him the emblem of the place. For months she had come and gone with trays of food while his mother was still ambulant, yet they had never exchanged a word. Sometimes, unasked, she would hand him a cup of tea. And as he drank it she would stand by his mother's bedside and simply watch. He felt in these moments that she was taking the burden of vigil from him, standing guard on his behalf, allowing him to rove away mentally. Free to consider other things – the birdsong in the dusk, the shivering of the trees.

What Stanley considered, though, was Irene, her solemn gravity, her vigilance. And after many months, her sheer familiarity. She became inextricably bound up in his mother's departure. He fretted secretly if she did not appear; as long as she was there the evil hour could be warded off. And she *was* there, right at the very end. By chance. Bearing away a jug of water which she had used on the useless flowers he brought. Standing at the foot of the bed, Irene recognised the signs. There was a moment before death when it seemed the world was holding its breath to inhale the dying one into the airy void. There it was, amidst all the noisy protestations – the battling, shallow breaths, the rasping in the lungs, the fevered twitching of fingers on the counterpane – a silence like the hesitancy before wonder. It was only by watching Irene that Stanley realised that his mother was about to die. It was her rapt attention which alerted him. An hour passed. A pallid hour of spring. She stood at the foot of the bed still holding the jug of water, the giver of life. The only move she made was to close his mother's eyelids with a benedictional grace.

The nurses came then, whipping the curtains angrily around the bed as if something untoward had occurred. They scurried back and forth intent on the business of disposal. Stanley, now an encumbrance, was asked to wait outside. The corpse, they said, must be prepared. He felt a stab of anger. All of this activity might have saved her instead of being expended now, when it was too late. He followed Irene out into the silent corridor. He had the impression that she had been waiting – for him. He had not planned to say anything, except perhaps to thank her, but for what he did not know. She had, in fact, done nothing but witnessed. But he remembered the raptured stillness of the hour they had just spent together, like a prayer, a contract already made between them. She watched him gravely as he reached for words.

'Don't leave me,' he simply said.

STANLEY GODWIN in the mortuary. The pungent smell of varnish, a wild glitter of brass. The coffin lid stood on its end. He ran his hands along the wood and knocked on it with his fist as if it was a doorway to another world. Behind him on a trestle lay his mother on a bed of unseemly satin ruffled regally at the neck. At his feet a scattering of shavings like the shorn kiss curls of children. In the mote-flecked entrance, the hearse's hatch-like yawn. And by his side, a girl he hardly knew who had shared his first hour alone in the world. It seemed inconceivable that he might lose her too. In his stiff white collar and funeral suit, within sight of his mother's remains (yesterday a corpse, today a remains), Stanley Godwin asked Irene to marry him. He was the last of his line. In the official records 'No issue' would be entered after his name. While his mother lived it had not troubled him. It was enough to know that the brief details of his life would be enscribed in stone beneath hers, a full circle. But with her gone Stanley felt for the first time the solitude of one who would not go forth and multiply. Like the last outpost of an empire, his memory would not outlast him. Up to this he had been the offspring, the bearer of possibility; without his mother, he was simply an ageing man, imprisoned in the cage of the seventy-odd years he could expect to live. His world was shrinking. The gift of Irene – he saw her this way, as an unexpected, undeserved gift – seemed to reverse that. She was a map stretching southwards, a window that afforded glimpses of the sea. She offered what he knew was impossible. New life.

Still in mourning, he took his new bride home. Death clung to him, whereas Irene, with years of it imprinted on her, shook Granitefield off with surprising ease. Or so Stanley thought. He watched fondly as she packed away her trinkets and keepsakes not realising that she was bringing with her the ghosts – and spoils – of dozens of other men. He did not register to their presence in the corridors of Granitefield, or see them lurking in the trees, shyly waving from the shadows. Nor did he know how important an escape this was for Irene. Free from the menace of Davy Bly, she could believe that her work here had been of value; it could remain mercifully intact. He did not notice how anxious she was to leave, now, straight away, nor how the only farewell that distressed her was Dr Clemens'. Wrapped in his broad embrace, she wept silently, burying her tears in the white starch of his generous shoulder, as he patted her companionably.

'There, there, my dear. No tears today! The world is waiting for you . . . you belong out there.' He released her and stepped back. 'You belong with the healthy and the strong.'

Irene watched him stride away down the grassy knoll towards the lake, proud, fierce and lonely. Like a beacon, he had always been there, a monumental presence. She could barely remember a time that did not include him, and the memories of the past to which he did not belong seemed so distant and intangible to her that they hardly mattered. At Granitefield, Irene's childhood had become a murky dream, a sort of pre-existence: it was *this* place that had borne her. And made her.

Grief-stricken, Stanley did not notice the gathering of phantoms. He suspected that in her low moments what

35

Irene missed was home, though he did not know where home was. She spoke little of the small port town in the far south where she had grown up. He knew that cargo ships docked there, and liners from the Mediterranean. Sailors and naval cadets swaggered on the quays. Rhododendrons bloomed in the gardens of the big houses – it was in the Gulf Stream. Emigrants started their passage there for the New World. Foreign tongues were common. A Turkish merchant sold sweetmeats from the Orient on the main street. A Jewish watchmaker fleeing from Poland had mistakenly disembarked there and set up shop believing it to be New York. It was a foreign country to Stanley. And he had brought her to this – a stony-faced imperial city, the clank and grind of shipbuilding. The light was thin and Nordic, the winds from the river hostile. And there was no joy on the Sabbath.

The big, hostile world that Irene had been afraid of for years turned out to be a small, terraced house on Jericho Street on the north side of the capital. The street seemed forbidding, two rows of red-brick houses baring teeth at one another, rising to a vertiginous height and blocking off the view of the city below. She compared it to the broader vistas she had come from, the dim perspectives of the institution, the sweep of corridors, the scale of penitential grounds. Used to roaming through the wards or sitting in the humming kitchens, she found Number 24 stifling and cell-like. The enclosure of it worried her – the shrunken rooms, the coal-dusted yard, the cloying proximity of neighbouring lives. The only concession to openness were the tiny patches of garden out front which ran into one another with no clear boundaries.

The tiny house oppressed her because it bore so keenly the traces of Stanley's recent loss. Only a place so mean could hang on to its owner so tenaciously, whereas Granitefield had lost so many that its large and airy wards could absorb the ghostly vestiges of its dead, and disperse them like dust motes floating in summer light. But here, the dead hand of Mrs Heather Godwin was everywhere. Not that she owned much. There was a meagre supply of cutlery and crockery, two large pots – one for stew, one for porridge – and a heavy, cast-iron frying pan. Everything had a place and a function. The hook on the back of the door where Mrs Godwin's apron still hung, a cubbyhole in the chimney breast for matches, a nail near the window for keys and bills owing. Irene had expected cosiness; instead there was a feeling of functional absence, and time marked slowly by the loud ticking of a wall clock. Yet, the paucity of utensils, the lack of pictures on the walls, the serviceable furniture, gave Irene a more acute awareness of Mrs Godwin than all the personal clutter she had expected.

Irene's idea of home was a place that could house a plethora of useless items. Cupboards for odds and ends, drawers full of bobbins and washers, tables and mantels groaning with decoration. But this sparseness unnerved her. It was as if Mrs Godwin was an absentee landlady who had made the place ready for new tenants but had not relinquished her hold. Indeed, Irene couldn't shift the notion that she might at any stage return, marching in with busy purpose, unhooking the apron from the back of the door (Irene dared not to touch it) and setting to with a duster or mop. She suspected that Stanley felt the same. He looked up sometimes when she came in and an expression she couldn't quite decipher would flit across his features. It was like a mild confusion as if he had forgotten which day it was, or as if he were unsure, just for a split-second, what Irene was doing there.

They shared what they both referred to as his mother's room. Gloomy and green, with a brown barque of a bed, it seemed always bathed in a dim, ferny light. For the first year, Irene lived out of a suitcase, draping her clothes on the back of a chair because Mrs Godwin's clothes hung in

37

the cavernous wardrobe. At one end of the mantel Irene carefully arranged her things – a brush and comb, hairclips, a hand mirror (this latter was a luxury; in Granitefield only the communal bathrooms had mirrors) and a jar of hand cream. After years of rough work in the kitchens only now did she feel permitted to look after her hands; now that she was a married woman. At the other end was Stanley's shaving brush and hair oil. Between them a dusty space which neither of them could populate. In their bed, too, as Irene was to discover. She would stretch her hand across the sheets touching Stanley's fleshy forearm. Her fingertips exploring the hollowed dimple that was his vaccination mark, travelling over his bare chest and down a serpent of hair to his clothed haunches. He would lie there, surrendering to her probing, his eyes averted as if she were conducting a humiliating, physical examination. He lay unmoved as she laboured. He was like a great liner weighing anchor and her efforts to please him like tiny streamers – primrose yellow, rose pink, cornflower blue – thrown from the deck, snapping as it pulled away. Irene, on the quayside, watched as they seeped into the murky shallows. Her life's work, the joyless skills of years, were of no use. Stanley Godwin was impotent.

DEFERENTIALLY THEY both withdrew; sometimes in the night Stanley would reach out for her tentatively, a flutter across her breast. But if Irene felt the blushing smart of her own desire she would damp it down. She had wished to be united in pleasure, not to be observed in it. The act of being looked at, at being done to, was weighed down with memories of Granitefield. She remembered the men she had saved. Their wanting, their yawning longing had always seemed to Irene more precious than the consummation which had expressed itself only as desolate relief, their moment of abandonment as functional as expectorating into the sputum jug beside their beds. She was glad that Stanley would never achieve this, the lonely spilling of seed and its death-like aftermath, the terrible spentness of it. It kept him apart from them; it made of him someone proud and unassailable, one who had secrets of his own he was not willing to share. She did not resent this. Rather, she fed on other tendernesses which Stanley offered, often unknowingly. His hand on the nape of her neck, the soft, burly strength of his embrace, his worshipping gaze. She loved the geography of his face, a country she had explored with her fingertips and the rough crevices of his blameless hands. She liked to watch him shave, the fluffy application of soap, the delicate dabbing of the shaving brush, the dangerous scrape of the cutthroat, his skilful mastery of jaw and cheekbone. When they went to church – she still did not believe but she went for his sake – she liked to link him on the street. It made her feel anchored, his bulk beside her steady and reassuring, a bulwark against the resistance she felt all around her.

She would always be a stranger here; the very street seemed to exhale disapproval. A brooding sense of violence seemed to seep from the bricks; at night she imagined she heard the pounding of troops on the slimy cobbles, the crashing down of doors, the seizure of captives in the dark. Stanley chided her; it was all in her head, he said. The neighbours hailed Stanley merrily when they were together but when Irene ventured out on her own she felt reproof and wariness in their greetings. She knew what they wanted from her – information, some means of placing her. A family name they could trace, a townland however distant they could ascribe to her. She was an unknown quantity among them and she knew that the only way she could counter that was to bear a child, whom they could claim as one of their own. The first thing they asked if they met her at the dairy or in the church porch was 'Any news?' By that, they meant one thing, the one thing Irene knew she could not deliver.

'Why do they torment us like this?' she would ask Stanley.

'They're just concerned, that's all.'

'They're just nosy, that's what you mean. Don't know how to mind their own business. Why can't they just let us be?'

Stanley would shrug and turn away. But as time went by he too began to dread the dogged enquiries after Irene's health. He would dodge neighbours on the street if he saw them first, longing for the simplicity of those years alone with his mother, a union without any expectations.

But away from their prying glances, Irene's presence, the very fact of her gave him courage. When she was not there he fell prey to a sense of foreboding, convinced she would not come back. If she travelled to the southside of the city, he imagined a catastrophe; a train crash; a murder. He felt oppressed in the backwash of her departures, surveying the cluttered house to reassure himself. She could not bear empty spaces. She had filled the rooms with all sorts of trinketry. Decorative plates adorned the walls, spotted delph sat proudly on the dresser. She had pinned pictures from magazines and cut-outs from greeting cards on the walls of the kitchen. Old calendars showing Alpine scenes still hung though their dates no longer had a bearing. She collected ashtrays, though neither of them smoked, souvenirs of places she had never been. Brighton, Inverness, St Helier. There was one without a declared place of origin, a gruesome object, molten-like, as if it had been boiled down from ghoulish droppings or lava. Greetings from Mount Etna, Stanley thought wickedly. She crocheted covers for things, cushions, tea cosies, even a pouch for the lavatory paper, as if everything must be disguised or dressed up as something else. The neighbours, he knew, considered the decor fanciful and further evidence of Irene's oddness. But he liked the busyness of it. It was like living in the stall of a bazaar; who knew what treasures lay hidden here? It was in this way he felt Irene had made herself known to him, substitutes for the small worries, the female confidences he had expected. Instead, she offered her delights – the anti-macassars, the doilies, the paper blossoms – with a girlish flourish. Their significance was lost on Stanley. Guiltily, he mistook them as shows of gratitude.

In years to come both Stanley and Irene, separated by distance and circumstance, would look back on the early years of their marriage as a surrogate childhood, a time on which the adult world had made no claim. He would recall the sense of protection she inspired in him, the telling gestures that indicated anxieties she would never speak of. He noticed how she examined her arms, fingering spots or exploring her wrist or elbows as if for bruises or marks of some kind. He felt she was looking for traces of illness, her old illness. She was conscious of the scar left by her operation and would always undress in the dark as if someone, other than him, was watching and would be shocked, though by then it was no more than a red seam on her flesh, like a light scrape with death.

Irene, in turn, would remember Stanley's softness, which in the harsh light of Granitefield she had determined as weakness but which she came to recognise as a kind of helpless power. She marvelled at what he allowed her to see of him, his fearfulness, his resigned acceptance of the world, even the absence of his desire. It seemed to her that all of these should have been hidden; for Irene what kept people intact was what they withheld. Her father, Dr Clemens – though she never considered them in the one breath – were understandable, one for his brutality, the other for his professional kindness, because by their nature they had achieved a safe, knowable distance. But Stanley occupied a place dangerously close to her; he entrusted her with knowledge she felt she shouldn't have. She worried that she might use it against him.

He was afraid of moths, she discovered. She came upon him in the bedroom one night, standing as if transfixed, while a moth flapped helplessly near the light bulb. He was stripped to the waist like a man about to do battle and it was only when she noticed his fingers clenched white around the collar of his shirt that she realised his terror. The moth was trapped behind the parchment shade. Its frantic clatter, the frenzied movements of a creature so small – it was inconceivable to Irene that this could be something to be afraid of. She was tempted to mock but something stopped her, some delicacy of the moment. She whipped the curtains closed and switched the light off. The mesmerising whirring ceased with the swift plunge into darkness, but Stanley still stood paralysed. She could sense the throb of his fear across the room.

'It's still in here somewhere,' he said. 'I can't sleep knowing it's here.'

So Irene would spend many daylight hours hunting away sleeping moths. How clever they were, she thought, melting grainily into wood, inhabiting the darkness and making it their own. Only the light fooled them; they threw themselves at it and betrayed themselves.

It was a hazy morning in April when Irene met Martha Alyward outside the Monument Dairy on the corner of the street. Irene had always considered her a rival. A flaxen-haired woman born in the same year, the mother of three schoolgoing sons. She had the knack of delicately prying into other people's lives. For Irene she was the epitome of Jericho Street – neat, tight-lipped, righteous. She fastened on to gloom, grimly watchful for the worst. An accident in the shipyard, a sick child, a drowning in the river. News of these invariably came through Martha who fed needily on the awfulness of the world.

'And how are we today?' Martha asked setting down two bulging bags of shopping. She took Irene in in one swift, critical glance. Irene had lost count of the number of times she had been surveyed in this fashion followed by the same sly inquiries and for Irene the inevitable humiliation of not being able to offer even the smallest of prizes. The pre-ordained pattern of it depressed Irene. She usually tried to avoid engaging Martha in conversation but sometimes, like now, it wasn't possible. She longed to be able to silence Martha, to shock her into submission, to get the better of her. The thought of such a victory made her suddenly giddy.

'I'm not the best, to tell you truth,' she offered cryptically.

'Oh?' prompted Martha.

Irene watched her expression change. A greedy curiosity replaced her usual pitying concern. Irene could not bear it. She pounced.

'I've been feeling queasy these past few mornings . . . '

'Oh?' Martha repeated.

Irene could smell blood; she was surprised at how easy it was. Martha needed only the vaguest implication.

'At first I thought I'd eaten something that disagreed with me. You know the way it is, you never think about the obvious . . . '

It was a moment of pure spite.

'You're not . . . ?'

Irene gloried in Martha's dumbfounded surprise. After four years, even she had stopped asking 'Any news?'

'Well,' Martha said finally, 'and when are you due?'

'November,' Irene said triumphantly.

'You'll have it in the Royal, I suppose?'

'Oh no,' Irene replied, moving away, 'I'll be going south.'

Stanley was the last to hear. Len Alyward stopped him on the street as he trudged home after the evening shift. He waved heartily from the bald patch that counted as his garden. He grew roses. Stanley was always amazed that anything would grow in the soot-laden air. Secateurs in hand, Len wandered across the street.

'Well, aren't you the boyo?' He laid a hand on Stanley's shoulder.

Stanley looked at him blankly.

'I knew you had it in you!' He nudged Stanley in the ribs. 'Oh come on, Stan, the whole street knows. You know what Martha's like. Bush telegraph!'

Len snapped the secateurs playfully. 'Congrats, old man, the first of many, eh?' He shook Stanley's hand. 'A celebration is in order, don't you think?'

Stanley frowned, still trying to figure it out. Len had always had the capacity to make him feel dull-witted.

'Give over, man, don't be coy! It isn't every day a man finds out he's going to be a father!'

From that moment, Stanley believed. Out of the mouth of Len Alyward, here on the dusty, weathered street, it just had to be true. They went to the Crown. Gold and gleam and the pour of liquor, ale that seemed to have taken on the colour of wood. The raucous jollity of the place – the crones in the snug, the scrums of dockers – convinced him that the whole world was in on the secret. The noises of their revelry danced in his fogged brain. He drank to prolong the moment of belief. After years of grounded loyalty, he felt the joy of the convert. The world had taken wings. He was no longer a rocky outcrop; he was joined, hip and heart. And Irene had made it possible, somehow.

It was two in the morning by the time he made it home. Irene, awake and fearful, heard his key in the lock. He fumbled with it several times before slotting it into place. He leaned heavily against the door after shutting it. Irene heard the pause as a gathering up of rage. She had seen it many times with her father, like the pawing of a bull before the charge. Her sense of victory over Martha had long since dissipated, giving way to a bleak panic. This lie, the calculated misunderstanding she had set in motion, would undo them both. It would strip everything bare. It would make visible the void at the centre of their marriage. And all the other deceptions would become obvious too. Stanley would know what she had become at Granitefield and would see it as Davy Bly had done, as a piece of whoring. She had thought of fleeing – she got as far as rescuing her suitcase from the attic – until she realised there was nowhere to go, and no man to save her.

She lay in bed listening to Stanley's heavy tread on the stairs, strangely exhilarated by the imminence of danger. When they were first together she had longed to be bruised by him, to have blue mottled marks on her thighs, love bites on her neck. A black eye, even. He entered the room, and sat heavily with his back turned to her on the other side of the bed.

'I met Len Alyward,' he offered, an explanation for his condition and the lateness of the hour.

Irene braced herself. She stretched out a hand to touch him. It was a conciliatory gesture but she fully expected the swipe of his fist in return. Instead he turned to her, his features blurred by drink bathed in an expression of almost beatific gratitude.

'I'm going to be a father,' he said.

It was Stanley who gave the child a name. It will be a girl, he declared with proud certainty, and she shall be called Pearl. Pearl had been his mother's second name, he explained, the one she had favoured herself. He was like a man bewitched, intoxicated with unexpected passion. So this, he thought, was what Rose Toper had felt when she would declare mournfully 'I love you'. It wasn't like walking on air, as she had said, it was like *being* air. He was in flight, a glorious, airy sensation. From his lofty height everything seemed steeped in munificence. The house, the street, the ghastly, jagged outlines of the city had become benign, withdrawing like respectful elders allowing them to luxuriate in their new-found joy. Even Irene seemed transformed. There was a curious grace in her movements now; he could see her thin, hard body, roundening and softening, and her watchful gravity becoming serene.

The new devotion Stanley lavished on her was the care Irene associated with a mother. It was the kind of love Stanley knew all about. He stopped her carrying coal in from the yard. He made her take naps in the afternoons. He worried extravagantly about her health. He would help her to rise from the low armchair in the parlour, placing his hand in the small of her back. In the evenings he came home with shop-bought cake. Basking in this new solicitude, she felt prized and cosseted as if she were a delicate, doomed child. To watch him during those months was to know what he would have been like had he been in love with her. His tenderness bloomed into something active and joyful, their marriage – for her, an escape, for him a need for shelter and protection – had become a right and fitting union. The child she had conjured up out of light and air had done all of this. Like a fairy or a sprite (no earthly child could have done it) she had waved a wand and granted them a wish. Irene wondered when he would call a halt to the make-believe while secretly hoping it would last just a little while longer, if only to delay the punishment she knew would inevitably come. And yet, in the midst of it, Irene imagined she could feel a stirring in her womb as if a little being was sprouting wings in there. Stanley would press his hand to her belly and believed that he felt something too. Between them they had formed a child destined to be lost. A pearl of great price.

It didn't last, of course, Stanley's flight. After three months of dizzying dislocation he fell to earth. It happened at the entrance to the shipyard. A light drizzle was falling. Summer seemed to have retreated behind a thicket of grey cloud. There was a large crash, the thump and boom of a girder falling to the ground from a crane that had been stealthily moving across his line of vision. A siren started wailing and there was the crunch of boots on gravel as men rushed to the scene. Matthew Earley, they cried, it's Matthew! Stanley stood, rooted to the spot. Above him the arm of the crane hung like the limb of a deformed god. The gaping belly of a liner with men crawling like insects over it, the agonised cries of the wounded one . . . and the spell broke. It was not Matthew Earley who lay pinned beneath a lump of iron, it was the coiled form of an infant, whom Stanley had been carrying for months. She disintegrated before his eyes, her smooth, glazed face like the remnants of eggshell trampled in the dirt. He stooped to pick a fragment up, something to remember her by, but there was nothing on the ground but tiny shards of glass and the stink in his nostrils of his own foolishness.

The miscarriage was announced at the beginning of the fourth month. (Irene had spoken of it too soon, the neighbours said quietly among themselves; she had tempted fate.) Stanley took Len Alyward aside one Saturday morning and said simply: 'We've lost it, the baby.'

'Bad luck, old squire,' Len said, 'but not to worry, there'll be others. Plenty more where that came from, eh?' He punched Stanley playfully on the arm.

Stanley felt a sharp pang of anger. He wanted to catch Len by the throat and throttle him. The idea of the child was festering inside him, poisoning him.

'She's not robust, you know,' he said evenly, 'Irene.'

It was one of her secrets, Stanley knew. Irene had taken great care to give the impression that she had worked at Granitefield but had not been a patient, for fear of being driven out again for being unclean. Len nodded sagely.

Galvanised by a rush of malice, Stanley went on.

'She may never go full term.' There, he thought spitefully, but it wasn't enough. 'It's the TB, you see, it's left a weakness.' Tellingly, he tapped his temple.

'IN THE MORNING, *when I raised myself to give my child suck, a dead child was there; and it was not till I looked at it more closely under the full light of day that I found this was never the child I bore. And when the other woman said, No, it is thy child that is dead, mine that is alive, she persisted in answering, Thou liest; it is my child that lives, thine that is dead . . . '*

It was only after their loss had been made public that Irene fell from grace. Not, she felt, for the untruth she had told but for failing to sustain the dream of a child. Stanley had believed and did no longer and he blamed her. As if *she* had the giving and the taking away of faith. She had created the child. She had fashioned it, a graceful phantom of light, but it was he who had nurtured it; his blinkered belief had made it flesh and blood. He had even given it a name, so that it had lost its wings and had fallen to earth. *He* had made it real. She had been a proud ship bearing a precious cargo; now she was a rusting bulk on the seabed. A woman who had lost *his* baby. And yet, it was he who had finished her off. Out there in the glare of his beloved street, he had wrung the life out of her with his big, bare hands. Irene looked, at his soft, dejected face, his palpable but unuttered grief, the honest grime of his toil and despised him.

Stanley felt himself finally to be alone in the world. The magnificence of his foolishness tormented him. His deepest longing, so secret that even he had not been aware of its power, had been exposed. It was in Irene's hands now and he could not trust her with it. He was appalled at how casually she had lied. It had simply come into her head, she said. What disturbed him was the malice in it, an intention to strike out not Martha, as she had claimed, but him, and the ease of it which spoke of a lifetime's practice. He had felt Irene to be his protection against the world; now there was menace in her companionship. He imagined she was mocking him, sneering at him behind his back. A ridiculous old man. He sensed her disenchantment, not like Rose Toper's baffled incomprehension, but something more unpredictable, as if she might do him harm. He did not know, if he ever had, what she was thinking. They shared the same bed but she would no longer touch him. He had long ago convinced himself of his own failure, but as long as Irene had not lost faith, there had still been hope, faint hope. Now she had taken even that away. Where once he had dreaded her advances and her fevered attempts to please him, he hungered now for even the merest brush of her fingertips.

A visitor arrived in the winter of that year. A visitor for Irene. In the five years they had been married no one known to Irene had darkened their doorstep. Stanley answered the peremptory tattoo of the knocker and opened the door to a wiry, handsomely dark young man. He had black, oily hair and a thicket of moustache. He was muffled up in a greatcoat, his hat brim tilted back rakishly. He was blowing on his hands and rubbing them together; his hot breath played briefly in the chilly evening. Two large cardboard suitcases stood at his feet and an order book was wedged under his armpit.

'We're not interested,' Stanley said.

Door-to-door salesmen were ten-a-penny. It wasn't a fit occupation for an able-bodied man, Stanley thought. These sort of men made their living preying on women. He was about to shut the door when Irene strayed into the hallway. She had been dusting in the front room and she held in her hand a small, blue, china bowl. Curiosity had brought her this far and she cocked her head to catch a glimpse of the stranger framed in the slice of light from the street. There was a shattering sound as the bowl fell unheeded to the floor. She clutched her apron in a bunch to her lips. She looked as if she had seen a ghost.

'Charlie Piper,' she murmured. 'Charlie Piper.'

The man let out a low whistle of surprise.

'Well, I'll be damned! As I live and breathe!'

Stanley stood awkwardly between them, guarding the threshold.

'Irene! Irene Rivers!'

Stanley registered her maiden name with a soft shock. He had always thought of her as simply Irene, an orphan in the world, without a past except for Granitefield which might well have spawned her.

'Why don't you come in?' he said, inching the door open.

The man struggled with the cases, shunting them into the hallway with his foot, then dusting his hands on his backside as he straightened. He started to unpeel his coat. He looked like a spiv, Stanley thought distastefully, scrutinising his cheap, creased suit, his unbuttoned shirt collar, the carelessly loosened knot in his tie.

'Surprise, surprise!' Charlie said jauntily. 'Cat got your tongue?'

Irene had not moved. She was aghast.

'I thought you were . . .'

'Typical!' he said turning to Stanley and winking broadly. 'She thought they'd put me six feet under.'

He thumped his chest victoriously. 'Listen to that! Clear as a bell!'

Stanley edged his way between them. He feared Irene was going to faint. She was swaying slightly as if the hall was the deck of a boat, and she was rolling with a gentle swell.

'This must be your old man, then,' he said extending a hand to Stanley. 'Charlie Piper at your service.'

She recovered enough to invite him into the parlour but it was Stanley who had to withdraw and make the tea; she seemed to have entirely forgotten her manners. As he waited for the kettle to boil, he could hear Charlie's boyish voice from the next room, full of congratulation. Stanley hovered in the scullery longer than he needed to, arranging the cups on the tray and after he had scalded the pot, gripping the steaming kettle in his hand. He felt the need to steady himself, as he might do if he were expecting bad news. He shook the thought away and fetching up the tray decisively marched into the parlour.

'Well, aren't you the wicked one!' Charlie Piper was saying as Stanley edged the door open with his foot and set the tray down. 'Running off with a visitor!'

So, thought Stanley, the connection was Granitefield.

'Irene's just been telling me, Stannie, how you two got hitched up.'

Stanley winced at the diminution of his name.

'Strictly against the rules, I can tell you! Fraternising they used to call it, isn't that right, Irene?'

He smiled saucily at Irene. She blushed and looked away. Stanley detected conspiracy.

'But then, Irene, you were always a special case.'

A special case. The phrase rankled, somehow. Stanley had always regarded Granitefield as a neutral place where intimacy would have no quarter. It was an institution, a factory of sickness and death. He had never thought of it having a secret, sensual life.

'And what about you?' Irene asked as she poured the tea. 'Sugar?'

'Oh, footloose and fancy-free, as ever! You know me, never had much time for settling down.'

You know me: Stanley tried to decipher meaning from Charlie's emphasis. 'As I was saying to Irene,

Stannie, after you've been in a place like Granitefield you never want to stop anywhere long enough to be caught again.' He balanced his cup and saucer carefully in one slender hand. He was painfully thin, Stanley noted.

'I tried to escape once,' he said bashfully. 'Did Irene tell you?'

Stanley shook his head.

'Nearly damned well killed myself in the process. And the thing is, you can never escape it, really. Am I right, Irene?'

Irene didn't answer.

'That place is in my bones, Stannie, I can tell you.' He sighed, then brightened. 'Still, it can't be all bad, can it? I mean it brought the two of you together!'

Stanley met Irene's gaze across the room. There was a pleading in her eyes. Don't spoil it, that look said.

'True,' was all Stanley could manage in response. But it was said heartily. Despite himself, he found Charlie's blatant optimism infectious.

'Any kids?' Charlie enquired.

'Yes,' Irene said promptly, 'but she's asleep right now.'

She pointed at the ceiling and put a finger to her lips. Alarmed, Stanley made to contradict her. There it was again, out of the blue. A totally brazen lie.

'She's nearly three months old,' Irene was saying. He realised with a pang that this was the age Pearl would have been. Her vengeance knew no bounds. He got to his feet hurriedly. Next Irene would be using her name; that was a cruelty he could not bear.

'Well,' said Charlie, taking the hint and also rising, 'I must be off! Nice to meet you folks!'

Irene fetched his overcoat from the hall.

'Good to see you again, Irene,' he said to her as he shrugged it on. 'Oh, I almost forgot . . . you'll *have* to see my samples now.'

53

She bought a remnant, a floral pattern, navy sprig on a white ground. It might make a cushion cover, she said idly, putting it to one side.

'Trust Charlie,' she said, 'never one to miss the chance of turning a quick shilling.'

Grudging and wry, it was not the tone Stanley expected. Not the way she might talk about an old flame. But why had she lied about the child? And why to *him*?

As if reading his thoughts, Irene said dreamily: 'He's the one who started all of this.'

Irene would remember this encounter as if it had been a brush with death. Or a relapse. A dangerous recurrence of the old disease. A sharp rise in temperature; a sudden collapse of the lung. He had no right, he had *no* right to reappear like that, no right at all. And with a great welcome for himself. Talking about old times, taunting her with his *bonhomie*, gloating. She could have lived a blameless life but for him.

It might have been Charlie's visit that prompted Irene to brood on her operation in Granitefield. She had not dwelt on the matter since she had left. But for the scar like a large fish bone traced on her skin, she would never have had to consider it at all. It was what they called an identifying mark. If she were dragged nameless from the river, that and her fillings would give her away. She could trace the route of the scar, fading though it now was, as surely as if she were sightless and reading Braille. If she were ever to have a baby – oddly, she considered the prospect more concretely since they had lost Pearl – it would mean another slashing of skin, a new wound. It would be by Caesarean; she knew this with a certainty she couldn't justify. No man had ever entered her; how could a baby come out? It would have to be torn from her, yanked out like her shattered ribs had been. What had become of those delicate shanks of bone removed so long ago, she wondered. Had they been stored in tall jars of formaldehyde like pickled ghosts? Or buried perhaps, a spindly quartet of ivory. Or had they been used, as Irene now suspected, to make something new. She saw a group of doctors, unknown to her, closeted away in a bubbling laboratory, grinding each rib down by hand into a fine dust. They would add something then. Using pestle and mortar. Milk, of course. Mother's milk. To make a paste as pliable as dough. And from that dough a baby make. A plaster-cast infant, glazed and prettied and cooked in the oven until hard. From dust and ashes, new life. This was her offspring, hers alone, the child of her illness, Irene's first loss. And she was still out there. Not dead, simply lost. In a hospital ward somewhere, unclaimed, waiting for her mother. This time Irene determined she would tell no one, not even Stanley. She would seek out the child who was rightfully hers, the fruit of Eve's ribs.

MAY BLESSED stood on the steps of the Four Provinces with the backs of her turned wrists resting on her hips like decorative jug handles. The VACANCIES sign on a pole lashed to the railings creaked rustily. Irene set her bag down and looked up hopefully at the buxom woman framed in the doorway.

'I'm looking for a . . . '

'Come in, come in,' Mrs Blessed interrupted, beaming. 'Plenty of room at the inn!'

She ushered Irene over the threshold and pushed the heavy front door to on a damp, mauve dusk.

'Mrs Blessed,' she declared. 'May Blessed.'

She gave her name as if it were tidings of great fortune.

'And you?' she enquired.

'Mrs North,' Irene said plucking a name from the air. A telephone jangled.

'Oh dear,' Mrs Blessed said letting her hand fall. 'No rest for the wicked!'

She disappeared through a glass-panelled door marked OFFICE.

'Four Provinces,' Irene heard her purr through the half-open door. 'Can I help you?'

Irene wandered out of earshot. Mrs Blessed had tried very hard to turn her rooming house into a hotel. There were little attempts at sophistication. The U-shaped reception desk padded in red vinyl, a latticed noticeboard for letters and announcements (the times of Masses), an umbrella stand. But inside the front door, left on the latch, dry leaves had gathered in rustling covens. A man's bicycle was propped up against the wall with a damp stain on the lino under the back wheel. Near the back stairs, a black call box was affixed to a pocked piece of chipboard embroidered with spidery names and numbers. A faint smell of stale fat hung in the air.

'Now, Mrs North,' said Mrs Blessed, emerging from the office. She lifted a large register and thumped it down noisily on the desk. 'How many nights?'

How many indeed. Startled into wakefulness in the small hours by a timid scratching from the other room, *her* room. Irene, bolt upright, would strain to read the night noises. She would shake Stanley.

'Do you hear it?'

She did not believe, as Stanley did, that it was the mating calls of toms that had roused her.

'What?' he would groan through a fog of sleep. (They joked about it at the yard when Stanley appeared hollow-eyed and dawny for work. Good night with the missus, eh Stan?)

'It's Pearl, listen!'

What he heard was the scrape and scurry of mice.

'Irene, Irene . . . ' Leaning on one elbow he would place a restraining hand on the crook of her arm, his only touch these days. 'You know that's impossible.'

And he would turn away, his broad, flannelled back a reproach. All his refusals were absolute.

'Mrs North?' Mrs Blessed repeated, calling her back.

Irene wished she wouldn't keep using her name like that. It was proprietorial, somehow, as if it was hers to bandy about, as if she had some claim to it.

'Oh, just the one.'

'Not from these parts then?' Mrs Blessed said as she penned Irene's name in the register. 'I detest a Southern accent.'

Irene shook her head.

'On a visit then?'

'Mm . . . yes,' Irene faltered. 'The hospital . . . '

'Nothing serious, I hope?'

'Oh no, not me. No, there's nothing wrong with me.'

'A friend, then?' Mrs Blessed prompted.

'Yes, that's right. She's just had a baby.'

'Isn't that nice! And you've come *all* this way . . . '

Was she being pleasant, Irene wondered, or just fishing.

'When I was having mine, I can't tell you how pleased I was to see my girlfriends,' she confided. 'I used to get weepy, you know. And men, men are no good at a time like that. I won't have a word said against my Eric, God rest him, but they just don't understand, do they?'

She turned and lifted a key from the rack behind her.

'Whereas *we* do,' Mrs Blessed said looking at Irene meaningfully, 'don't we?'

Irene blushed with a secret pride; she had been mistaken for a mother.

'Number two, I think.'

'No, no, it's her first one.'

Mrs Blessed chuckled.

'We seem to have our wires crossed. I'm putting you in room number two.'

'Home sweet home!' Mrs Blessed said, throwing open the door of number two with a flourish.

They had travelled to the top of the house, up several flights of stairs carpeted in whorled crimson, geese flying in formation on the flocked fleur-de-lis wallpaper, a gilt tureen housing an asparagus fern on the return. None of it had prepared Irene for this barren interior. It was a white attic room, long and narrow, with a window at the far end under which two single beds were wedged, a locker squeezed between them. The timbered ceiling which sloped to one side had once been painted but it flaked and blistered now as if afflicted by a leprous disease. There was a curtained cavity for clothes. Over the bricked-up fireplace a picture of the Virgin hung.

'It's really for two, as you can see,' Mrs Blessed said, bending to smooth one of the pink candlewick spreads. 'But in your case, I won't charge.'

In your case. Irene pondered on this.

'My radio officers were in here, bless their hearts. Lovely lads. But my, what a racket they made. They used to practise their Morse code at the table, clinking their spoons against the cups. Sending messages to one another, if you don't mind!' She folded her fat arms.

'Now,' she said, 'rules of the house!' She tapped a notice which was tacked to the back of the door. 'The Ten Commandments, I call them! No baths after ten, bathroom's across the landing, and no men in the rooms, but I'm sure I don't have to tell you that.'

She fidgeted briefly with the waistband of her skirt as if she longed to inch the zip down just a fraction.

'Breakfast at eight sharp and we like our guests to vacate by nine.'

She turned to leave, worrying at a stray strand of hair that was curling around her earlobe.

'Oh yes, I nearly forgot. The front door is locked at midnight. I tell my girls I only keep Cinderellas!'

And with a merry laugh, she retreated.

An hour later, dodging Mrs Blessed, Irene slipped out. She knew the hospital was close by – it was why she had chosen the Four Provinces – and she wanted to see it, just from the outside. From the step she could see its jigsaw of roofs and gables, and the dome of a copper cupola rising above them. She prowled around the perimeter of the building. It took up almost a block. There was the lullaby hum of a generator somewhere in its juggled heart, and steam gasping from the laundry into the dark night. It was pot-bellied in front, bulging into a pillared rotunda, as if the builders had vainly tried to fence in its fecundity. Irene sheltered in a pub doorway opposite the entrance and watched as visitors streamed through its portals. They were mainly fathers, some with children, ham-fistedly attired, buttoned incorrectly into their coats. Even temporary motherlessness seemed to give them an unkempt, woebegone look. Irene was loath to leave her vantage point. Like a woman bewitched by the house of love she examined the sooted curves of the portico, each lighted window.

Her child was in there, after all, and this place would become part of her history, however briefly. Some day Irene would have to describe this – the raw night, the soft drizzle leaving a glistening film on her cheeks. Her hair lay damply on her forehead. The wet, chilly air made her seem oddly feverish. Was this a maternal bloom, an anxious glow on the eve of birth? Or was it the old disease come back? At that thought, she pulled the collar of her coat up and hurried back to the Four Provinces.

'How's your friend, Mrs North?' Mrs Blessed called out cheerily as Irene pushed the front door open gingerly. She was bent over her books at the desk, worrying over calculations, her mound of black hair just visible over a red tasselled lampshade. Irene had hoped to get past without having to engage in conversation.

'She's fine, thank you, just fine.'

'And the baby's doing well?'

Irene hovered at the foot of the stairs, one hand on the banisters.

'Boy or a child?'

'Pardon?'

'Is it a boy or a girl?'

'Oh, it's a little girl,' Irene replied. 'Pearl.' She bit her lip; she must be careful.

'What a pretty name . . . oh, look, you're soaked through. Here, take those wet things off. What you need is a nice cup of tea to warm you up.'

'No, really, it's quite alright,' Irene protested.

But there was no arguing with Mrs Blessed. So Irene surrendered to her blandishments. She was ashamed of the effect such random kindnesses had on her. She did not understand how a hand on her shoulder or a man opening a door for her could bring unbidden tears to her eyes. She would bat them away feeling foolish and monstrous. It wasn't as if she weren't loved. Momentarily, as she sat in Mrs Blessed's warm kitchen sipping the welcome tea, she remembered Stanley. If he knew . . . she shook the thought off. Mrs Blessed mistook it for a shiver.

'There, you see, you've got a chill.'

She must not succumb to any muffling tenderness she might still feel for Stanley, Irene thought, as Mrs Blessed threw a warm towel around her shoulders and dried the wet ends of her hair. She was doing this for him too.

Irene did not unpack her things. She wanted to leave no trace. She sat on one bed, and then the other, testing the springs. Both sagged in the middle, worn into an accommodating hollow by the sleep of strangers. The austerity of the room reminded her of Granitefield, where only illness had a personality so that the white bedsteads and lockers, the regulation counterpanes and curtain screens, had a dogged neutrality. They refused to be owned. The noises of the house reached her through the thin walls. The squeal and rush of a toilet somewhere below, the gurgling of a cistern. The thud of a door. The pock of a light switch. A gargler in the bathroom. She tried to visualise the other guests but all she could come up with were identikit pictures, a juggled collection of cruel noses, narrowed eyes, thin, twisted smiles. She did not wish to meet any of them. She listened intently at her door before opening it and crossing the landing to the bathroom. It was a large, draughty room painted an icing blue. All the fixtures were at one end like a capsizing ship. It catered for the cleansing of several bodies not intimate with one another. A few gnarled knobs of soap lay in the wire tray over the bath. There was a green stain under one of the taps like the ghost of a waterfall. The beaker clamped to the mirror above the basin, which should have held a cheery array of toothbrushes, was empty and foul-smelling. The ill-tempered geyser shuddered noisily into action when she turned it on, issuing a jet of boiling water into the sink and sending clouds of steam wafting towards the ceiling. The mirror became opaque. Irene stood in the seamless fog, her hands pale and blameless beneath the still surface of the water, and felt cleansed. Forgiven. It was not too late for her. An impatient rattling of the door knob shattered the moment. Hurriedly she splashed her face. She brushed her teeth fiercely. Then, furtively checking at the door, she slipped back across the landing and into the haven of number two.

She undressed self-consciously. She couldn't remember the last time she had disrobed in a room where no one was looking. As she climbed into bed she caught a glimpse of the small patchwork of city visible through the thinly curtained window – the lapping slate roofs, a trio of chimney pots, puddles in the valleys, the splutter of a broken drainpipe streaming heedlessly below. She was naked; there was nobody to see her. The feel of her own unobserved skin next to her was strange and lurid. She stroked the crowns of her nipples; she sought the cleft of moisture between her legs. A shiver of joy made her gasp. She was, at last, invisible.

The morning had a glowering air, a sulky, hangover feel. Seagulls swooped, brayed and scattered. Irene wrinkled her nose at the smell, from the brewery, she guessed, yeasty, like chicory. Street hawkers passed her pushing prams stacked with pyramids of apples glistening from a dawn shower. A few grizzled old men stood listlessly in doorways dragging on flattened butts. A street sweeper gathered armfuls of wet leaves and deposited them lavishly in a barrow. The dismal streets made her melancholy, reiterating her sense of homelessness. It was only eight-thirty and she had several hours to kill. She felt resentful at having been turned out of the Four Provinces after breakfast. House rules indeed! They just didn't want her here. She turned on to Gloucester Street. She made a mental note of it. She could not afford to get lost. If she did she might have to ask for directions and they would know she was a stranger. Afterwards somebody might remember. In fact, nobody remembered the gaunt woman in a black beret and severely belted maroon coat and rubbed-looking gloves with a pearl at the wrists. The girls playing piggybeds among the peelings or swinging languidly from a lamppost barely looked up as she wandered, like a careful ghost, through the battered landscape of their games. It was the season for skipping. Thwack of rope and a strange, sour chanting. Or they stood idly in twos and threes chewing the split ends of their hair as Irene threaded her way through them, intent only on their own whispered secrets. There were small boys crouched in knots over games of marbles, their mittens sewn with elastic to their hand-me-down coats. They seemed in thrall to the glassy baubles shot through with seams of ochre and Prussian blue and would have registered Irene only as another pair of mottled female legs passing by.

A bald infant propped up in a large, spoked carriage on the path gnawed on a dummy and watched her solemnly. She was the only one to meet Irene's eye. For a brief, mad, moment she considered lifting the child out, so grateful was she for this trusting gaze. She could dance the baby in her arms as she had seen other women do quite naturally. As she stood there a lorry rattled past with three boys hanging from the back.

'Scut behind, Mister!' someone shouted out.

Startled, Irene turned around thinking that she would find a grimy child pointing a finger at her. Then she checked herself; she had done nothing. Yet. The lorry screeched to a halt and a beefy driver leant out the window. The boys leapt off nimbly and scattered. The driver lumbered from his cab and made a vain attempt to chase them. Then he gave up and with a loud curse and a fist waved indiscriminately in the air, he heaved himself aboard the cab and drove off. Though Irene had stood transfixed, the incident had barely caused a ripple on the street. She found herself gripping the handle of the pram. And then she noticed with relief that the baby was strapped in with a pair of reins. She was safe. Quite safe.

Irene turned back. From the brown hallways of the tenements she could hear the clangour of plumbing and the slop of laundry in tin baths. At the doorways young women gathered, slovenly and insolent to Irene's eye. 'Holy Jesus . . . ' she heard one swear. Another broad-beamed, plump of breast and heavily pregnant, was confiding mirthfully: 'Gene only has to *look* at me, know what I mean?'

'Pius?' a red-haired woman roared, wiping her hands on her apron. 'Pius!' A whey-faced toddler looked up from the gutter.

Irene hurried on glad that *her* child was not going to be brought up here.

IF MICHAEL CARPENTER had not hanged himself, Mrs Blessed might have made the connection between the Baby Spain kidnap and Mrs North but the violence perpetrated in the Four Provinces drove all else from her mind. She had only noticed something was amiss when the top bathroom was engaged for over an hour, a gross violation of the house rules. It was a Saturday morning. She allowed her regulars to sleep in at the weekends if they were prepared to forgo breakfast. Usually it was no sacrifice; sore heads were the order of the day. She didn't reach the top of the house until ten forty-five (that's how she put it when the police asked; it sounded more official that way and also gave the impression that she timed her household chores). The bathroom door was locked. She knocked and tried the handle.

'Anyone in there? Hello?'

There was no response.

'Hello?' she ventured again.

The lock had always been faulty; there had been trouble with it before. All it had taken then was a quick jiggle of the knob. Mrs Blessed tried again. Long years as a landlady had sharpened her instinct for trouble; she knew there was somebody in there, but *who* she could not work out. She made her way downstairs; she would check the register. By a process of elimination she could work it out. On the landing below she bumped into the commercial traveller in number six. She had a soft spot for him. He had been

65

staying at the Four Provinces on and off for years. A real card, he was, though fond of a drop. He looked a bit rough this morning. When this mess was sorted out she would take him into the kitchen and give him a feed.

'What's the problem, Mrs B?' he asked noticing her air of preoccupation.

'Top bathroom. Locked or stuck, I don't know which.'

'Let me take a look at it.'

He bounded up the stairs two at a time. She heard him put his shoulder to the door. There was a sharp splintering of glass as he smashed in one of the frosted glass panels.

'Holy Jesus,' she heard him gasp.

She hurried up the stairs, imagining a domestic disaster, a burst pipe or the bath overflowing. She always felt a mild panic about these alarums and the acute absence of a man about the house.

'I don't think you should go in there, Mrs B,' the traveller said pulling the bathroom door to.

Mrs Blessed caught a glimpse of a pair of hairy legs and Michael Carpenter's bloated member. She blessed herself swiftly.

Michael Carpenter was one of Mrs Blessed's radio officers. To her he was a happy-go-lucky boy with a black mop of curly hair and a bridge of freckles across his nose, whose only sin was to wear his socks in bed. She would find them in the mornings, lost among the sheets, and would have to open wide the window to rid the place of their vile smell. He wolfed his food, mopping up after his fry in the mornings with handfuls of extra bread (strictly rationed in Mrs Blessed's establishment). But beyond his healthy appetite she had noticed nothing, nothing to account for *this*. She did not realise that he used his socks to masturbate into. Nor that he and Conway (they always called one another by their surnames; it was a form of intimacy) indulged in half-naked horseplay in their room that stopped just short of buggery. Conway had a girlfriend which meant that he would not go all the way. He had gone to visit her that weekend leaving Carpenter to that particular boredom of the young in rented accommodation. It was a furtive kind of indolence, a lethargy in search of oblivion. He had heard somewhere – probably in the lavatories at the naval college – that a constriction around the neck enhanced erection. With a fetishist's care he had bought a length of washing line several weeks previously in a hardware store in the city. As he fastened a knot around the skylight in the bathroom, he remembered entering the shop past the mournful clanking of the buckets, bins and watering cans hung up outside.

'How many feet will she be wanting?' the man behind the counter had asked, presuming that the washing line was for the young man's mother.

Michael climbed up on to the chair he had brought from his room, testing to see if the rope would hold. He was pleased with the result. Knots were his speciality, after all. The bath was running as he did this, to disguise the sounds of his labour. He checked the lock on the door once more, then undressed quickly in the foggy room and climbed, shivering, on to the chair. Despite the steam, his skin bristled. He tugged on the rope once more then slipped the noose he had fashioned around his neck, and tightened it. He braced himself, then out of habit made a brief sign of the cross before stepping out into mid-air. As he did, Irene Godwin, tried the handle of the door outside. He saw a woman's outline through the dimpled glass and scrambling to regain the chair, his legs wheeling, he tipped it over with his right heel. He watched with horror as it keeled over. The blood rushed to his loins and flailing and kicking, eyes bulging with disbelief, Michael Carpenter had the biggest orgasm of his life.

Mrs Blessed searched in vain for a note. It gave her an excuse to rummage through his belongings. She was certain there was a girl involved, she told the police. Maybe he had left something in code.

'In code?' the detective asked.

'You know, dots and dashes,' Mrs Blessed explained obligingly.

'Morse, you mean?'

'Yes, he used to send messages to his friend, spoons on the teacups.' The detective shut his notebook resignedly. The world, he was convinced, was going mad.

A familiar combination of smells assailed Irene's nostrils when she entered the hospital just after eleven. Ether and floor polish. She inhaled it deeply, savouring the lostness of the memories it evoked. The lift beckoned. She hesitated before taking it; confinement frightened her. But she wanted to act, to do the deed as quickly as possible. She stepped inside, noting the three other occupants, an elderly man, a mother and a small child. She kept her eyes on the floor, firm in the belief that if she didn't look at them she would remain invisible. The young woman yanked the metal grid closed. The lift whirred and they began to move, edging slowly upwards. A red spot of light winked above the door. The boy, no more than three Irene guessed, was mesmerised by it, his large blue eyes fixed on it as if he were transfixed by a vision. Irene willed the flashing light to travel faster and as she did there was a sickening lurch and they were plunged into darkness. The lift swung airily between floors. Irene, pinned in the corner, saw in her mind's eye the vertiginous lift shaft. She imagined that all that was keeping them aloft was a series of frayed ropes and creaking pulleys like a cradle teetering on a fissured branch. She held her breath, afraid that any false move of hers might send them crashing down. In the dimness she could only barely make out the furry silhouettes of strangers. She caught the rank smell of her own fear. The woman jabbed angrily at the button near the doors, then banged on the metal grid.

'Help!' she bellowed.

Irene felt something cold and sticky brush against her skin. She stifled a scream imagining some gelid discharge running down the walls of the lift as a result of the jolt, but it was only the child seeking out his mother's hand in the darkness. Irene took it gratefully. The woman thumped on the bars of their cage a second time. The lift shuddered again like a beast wakened from slumber. There was a whine and they were off, thundering down the shaft, clanking and squealing – afterwards Irene couldn't tell if their voices had joined in with the machinery's protesting wails – before landing on the ground floor with a jarring thud. Another safe arrival. They tumbled out gratefully into the dazzle of daylight, Irene leading the little boy by the hand until he looked up and, realising that she was not his mother, swiftly withdrew his hand and spat on his palm.

She made for the stairs. Maternity was on the third floor. At the entrance to the ward there was a linen closet with its door slightly ajar. Irene slipped inside and locked the door. She set her bag down. She took off her hat and coat, hanging them on the back of the door. All around her were piles of newly starched linen, among them a number of white coats. She did not consider this lucky. There was no luck involved here. She took it as her due, as proof of the rectitude of her mission, the fruit of her long years of apprenticeship at Granitefield. She was an explorer who, having studied the maps, finds the terrain corresponds with the cartographer's drawings. This was her territory; she could have reached her destination blindfold.

Coat flapping, she stepped out into the corridor and, pushing the swing doors briskly, she entered the ward.

Two nurses gossiping over a trolley of medicaments were aware only of a flash of white as she swept by. On her right she saw the nursery. It was a long, bright room with an aisle down the centre between the rows of cots. She moved towards the door which stood invitingly half-open. Gingerly she stepped inside. For a moment, standing there in the glass-walled room she felt totally exposed, a predatory fish gliding menacingly in a bowl. She braced herself. She mustn't lose her nerve now. Wrapping the white coat around her for protection she walked boldly between the serried rows of cots. They were empty; they were all empty. It must be feeding time she realised with a sharp pang. She was about to turn and flee, smarting at this lack of foresight when she spotted right at the very end of the room a little pink mound. A little girl – she knew from the colour of the blanket – *her* little girl. Heart pounding, she made for the distant cot. She leaned over the sleeping baby. How peaceful she looked. It seemed a shame to disturb her. Irene, clutched by terror but greedy with desire, froze. If the baby were woken she would surely cry and that would draw attention. Or would it? Babies must cry all the time here. Their plantive whimpers must be part of the tapestry of the place. Panicked, Irene looked about her. A young man, a father she guessed, was peering in through the glass at her. She turned her back on him swiftly and found herself bathed in the green gaze of a newly-born. Pearl!

She hesitated no longer. This was her child, the only one here without a mother. She stooped and gently gathered Pearl in her arms, swaddling the pink blanket around her. She pressed her lips to Pearl's downy head. Her fontanelle fluttered in time to Irene's racing pulse. They were as one. She threaded her way carefully back, through the open door, and past the young man who was still peering in at the window with a puzzled look like a man who has lost something. Down the sheeny corridor, through the swing doors – Irene anticipated each step of the journey – and then a sharp left into the haven of the closet where she, no, they (it was the first time Irene had thought in the plural) would be safe.

She almost dived for the closet and once inside with the door safely locked she leant against it for several minutes, hugging Pearl to her. She felt weak. There was a sticky film of sweat on her brow. Calm, calm, she told herself, it is not over yet. She switched on the light and made a bed for Pearl in a nest of towels. From her bag she drew out a blanket and discarding the regulation pink wrapped this around Pearl. She peeled off the white coat and flung it in a corner. Hurriedly she put on her own coat, stuffing her beret into the pocket. She looped the bag around her wrist and then carefully gathered Pearl in her arms.

'Shush there,' she whispered.

But there was no need. Pearl, her knotted face nuzzling at Irene's breast, was adrift in sleep, her tiny fingers curled at her ears.

Irene edged the door open. Through the slit she could see a knot of people gathered at the lift. An orderly slouched over an empty stretcher, one of the gossipy nurses fingering stray wisps of hair escaping from her starched cap, an elderly couple, the wife clasping the man's hand, for balance not for love. She tried to imagine her own parents now, wondering how they had aged, but all she could see was the high tower and the steady warnings, a pattern of light and shade. William and Ellen Rivers. She used their proper names now as if they were but distantly related.

She inched the door almost closed and waited for the screech of the lift. It came and went. She waited. There could perhaps be visitors loitering outside, disgorged from the lift, lost travellers in a foreign country unsure of which road to choose. She heard the slap of the swing doors to the ward. She peered out again. On the threshold she found an easeful lull she recognised, a mid-morning hush. She remembered it from Granitefield. Dust swirling in the weak light, the throbbing stillness of a building holding its breath as if waiting to be stormed. These were sacred moments as in a silent church aquiver with candlelight. Sacred but short-lived. Irene stepped out on to the corridor and walked with purpose to the stairwell.

Only one person passed as she tripped down the stone flights, a nun, head bowed. Irene would remember only a swish of serge, the clack of beads, the stiff rebuke of a wimple. She, on the other hand, would have no memory of Irene, lost as she was in some vague thought of God. Irene made for the river. A clamour of black-nosed traffic greeted her, the rickety shrill of bicycles. The bridge beckoned. Alabaster over green. Soon, soon, they would be safe.

STANLEY GODWIN opened the door of 24 Jericho Street on a stormy Saturday afternoon to find Irene standing there, a pitiful creature in the rain, laden down. Shopping, he thought resignedly. Her rare trips south were invariably marked with untypical extravagance. This time, she had told him, she was going back to Granitefield, to revisit old haunts; he had not expected her back so soon. A taxi throbbed on the street behind her.

'Would you pay him?' Irene asked him, gesturing to the driver who was standing on the kerb with a coat over his head to protect him from the downpour.

'I didn't have enough,' she said as she brushed past him. It was only then he saw the baby and it was such a fleeting glimpse – a notion of a downy head, a tiny fist – that he wondered if his eyes were deceiving him. Sometimes, when he was exhausted, he would close his eyelids and find in his new blindness the exploding fragments of his last waking memory. It was a trick of the mind, he decided, a purblind vision of the phantom child they had lost.

'Right, chief?' the driver called.

Stanley dug into his pockets.

A well of silence greeted him when he shut the door.

'Irene?' he called from the foot of the stairs.

He placed his foot on the bottom step but was frightened to proceed any further. There were times when Irene could conjure up a dark mood out of thin air.

'Boil some water,' she shouted.

'Irene, what's going on?'

He could hear her rummaging in the spare room. Pearl's room. She was pulling out drawers, drawers he knew that were filled with baby clothes and stacks of nappies she had bought when . . . There was a cot in there, always made up as if a baby might at any time arrive out of the blue.

'Irene,' he called out again.

And then he heard it, unmistakably, a baby's cry. He hadn't dreamt it up. An old joy stirred in him but he stifled it.

'Irene,' he called testing out his voice against the phantoms. And then, resignedly, he did as he was bid.

He lit the fire in the parlour. The rain lashed against the window but Irene and the baby were heedless to the noisy inclemency of the weather. He watched them and felt as if he did not exist, except as a notion, a thought not materialised. He was afraid to go near in case the picture might disintegrate. He feared if he did that he would wake up and find he had been seeing pictures in the blue and gold flames in the grate. He rushed to and fro, setting the baby's bottle at Irene's feet, warming water in the tin basin and placing it in front of the hearth. He tested the water with his elbow; just tepid, Irene had said. He spread out a bath towel and drew back as Irene unswaddled the baby. She lay it out on the towel and free of its encumbrances it kicked and waved its arms, its eyes thrown back, attracted to the shimmering glow of the fire. With a soft shock he realised it was a girl child.

For as long as the baby was there, there was no need for either of them to speak. The child was all. Stanley noticed Irene's deftness as she stroked the child's silken skin and plashed the water gently round its head. There was something supple and reassuring about her movements; he felt a twinge of jealousy. This surety of touch had once included him. He was reminded of his own mother carding wool before this very fire with the same knowing serenity. And he realised that once, so far back that he couldn't remember, such care must have been lavished on him. He watched Irene as she touched the baby's tiny fingers, gently rubbing the wrinkless that would become knuckles and the fingernails which were like delicate slivers of mother-of-pearl. She traced around the little hump of her forehead, her hairless brow knitted, as if even sleeping required the utmost concentration, her button nose, the perfect cleft above her puckered lips. There was a strawberry-coloured mark on the baby's chin, a raised luscious bump, a fruity blemish as if she had been picking berries in that other place from which she had so recently come.

At six, Irene went upstairs and put the baby to bed. Stanley could hear her overhead. A loose timber creaked as she moved back and forth, singing quietly to the child and hushing her with a threatening kind of tenderness. He dreaded Irene's return alone. He wanted the spell to continue. The anxious father resting before the fire, the attentive mother singing lullabies to her baby above, and all around him the indisputable evidence of a new life – the bottle, the tin bath, the little clothes, a stray bootee. He heard her step on the stair. A terror gripped at his throat. He both wanted to know and was frightened of finding out the price of their newly born happiness. Even in a few short hours, the baby had bound them together. It gave a logic to their existence, sharing this house, living as man and wife. If he could have stayed silent, he would have. Silences between them were nothing new, after all. But he couldn't. As she entered the room, he cleared his throat.

'Don't ask,' she said.

'But, Irene, please . . . '

75

'It's better if you don't know.'

She sank into a chair opposite him and picked up from the floor one of the child's things, a pink blanket. She played with its satin-edged hem.

'Where did the baby come from?'

'I found her under a cabbage leaf.' She laughed grimly.

'Irene, *tell* me.'

'It's Pearl, Pearl has finally come home. And this time she's mine, all mine.' Her eyes glinted fiercely in the firelight.

'What do you mean?'

'You killed her off, remember, my first one?'

'Irene, whose child is it?'

She sighed and bit her lip thoughtfully.

'Irene, for God's sake . . . '

'It's Charlie Piper's,' she said finally.

'Charlie Piper?' There was a taste of bile in his mouth.

'He came back . . . '

'You mean it happened *here*?' He rose slowly. 'And all these months . . . '

'Yes,' she said bitterly, 'all these months and you noticed nothing.' She stared at him stonily.

He cursed himself. He had been so preoccupied with phantoms he had been blind to the truth.

'Do you love him?'

'He had something I wanted.' She corrected herself. 'He had something we wanted.'

He lunged at her, moving so quickly that for a moment she thought something had fallen on her, as if the ceiling had suddenly given way. He struck her across the cheekbone once and then again on the upstroke. His face was taut with anger, shiny as a death mask. He tore her dress from shoulder to waist, then flung her against the wall. The pink blanket slithered to the floor. She reached out for it but he stamped on her wrist with his foot. She struggled to rise. He pushed her down and sat astride her. The flames played on his face, turning his eyes to dark shadows. He spat at her. She could feel his spittle running down her face. He spat, and spat again.

'Whore,' he snarled at her. 'Whore.'

She turned her face away and shut her eyes tightly. She tried to wriggle a hand free to ward him off but he had her manacled now, her right cheek pressed against the skirting. And then, from above, she heard Pearl crying. That was all she heard, the child sobbing, as Stanley tore down her stockings and yanked at her underwear. She swung wildly at him with her free hand as he unbuttoned himself and entered. It was merciless. He laboured, sawing at her like a log he was trying to split in two. He came in one huge spasm, a terrible trembling in his limbs before he fell on her, a dead weight. And then he heard it too, the child's cries. He rose and blundered out of the room. His daughter needed him; he must see to her.

Irene did not stir. She lay there, motionless, a woman almost dead, semen on her thighs. She touched her bruised cheek. Her eyelid was already closing. She imagined how it would be in the morning, puffed up with a plum-blood bruise on the rim of the bone. She let her eyes wander around the defiled room, the toppled chairs, Pearl's scattered things, the dying fire. It was a child's eye view; the drawn curtains yawned above her, the standard lamp tall as a building, the sofa solid and safe as a pier. She must have lain there for an hour or more, while above her Stanley crooned to the baby, rocking her in his arms as he paced with her. A blessed darkness overtook her. After several hours the coldness of the room summoned her back; the fire's embers were dying. Numb and stiff, she rose, pulling the torn fragments of her clothes around her. All was quiet; the house was at peace. She caught a glimpse of herself in the mirror above the mantelpiece. A half-crazed creature, hair wild and matted and a wound on her face. She touched it gingerly and smiled weakly. She had finally been punished. Punished for all the things Stanley did not know about her. Everything would be alright now.

A CHILD ANSWERED the door to Charlie Piper. Her hair, parted in the middle, was tied in pigtails; her eyes when she peered up at him, were hazel. She wore a puzzled expression, her brow knitted into two tiny wings. There was a birthmark on her chin. It struck a chord with Charlie. Then he thought of Gloria, the telephonist at Granitefield, the one with the sexy beauty spot. This one, he thought, would also grow up to be a heartbreaker.

'Hello there!' Charlie leaned down and took one of her sticky hands. She made to withdraw but he held firm.

'Ah now, don't be like that, this is your Uncle Charlie!'

'Who is it, Pearl?' someone called from the interior. Charlie recognised Stannie's voice.

'It's Uncle Charlie,' she shouted.

Charlie searched through her features for some resemblance to Irene but couldn't find any. Must take after the other side, he thought.

Stanley, in vest and braces, coming to the door, saw above his tow-headed girl the inevitable future, the defeat he had always known was in store. But even then, he thought he could ward it off. He and Irene had protected this child with a ferocity borne of the very danger there was in having her and the fear, unspoken between them, that she might one day be taken from them. It was Irene, who, after weeks of keeping Pearl a secret, had told Martha Alyward that the child was adopted, an unwanted baby, the product of sin. Stanley had been astounded by her

79

insouciance; she had said this without flinching. And yet he knew why; it was as much to punish herself as him. Pearl was a well for both of their sunken secrets. And the one person who could threaten all of this was standing in front of him.

'Stannie!' Charlie rose from his hunkers. 'How goes the war?'

'What do *you* want?' He placed a protective hand on Pearl's shoulder.

These Northsiders, Charlie thought, dour lot, too direct for his liking.

'Just a social call,' he said dropping the child's hand. He felt somehow as if he had been caught doing something improper. 'No samples, this time, I promise.' He laughed nervously. 'Irene about?'

'What do you want with her?'

Charlie, used to resistance on the doorstep, ignored Stanley's hostile tone. He wondered vaguely what ailed the man.

'So this is the little girl I didn't see the last time,' he said chucking Pearl under the chin. 'You must be nearly six, is that right?'

'No,' the child said stoutly, 'last week was my birthday. I was four.'

'Aha!' Charlie said, 'already telling lies about her age. They start young these days, eh Stannie? Then it must be your sister I'm thinking of. Last time I was here she was only a babby, and that's coming up to six years, would you believe?'

It was the blatancy of this lie that enraged Stanley, the sheer bare-facedness of it.

'You can't have her, she's ours now, we've made her ours, do you understand?'

He pushed Pearl behind him. She started to wail.

'Steady on there, Stannie, what's all this about?'

'If you as much as lay a finger on her, I'll throttle you, understand?'

Stanley stepped belligerently out on to the street. Charlie took a step back and raised his hands but not in time to fence off Stanley's first blow which landed squarely on his chin. He staggered backwards and Stanley landed a fist in his lungs (Charlie's weak spot). He fell, winded, the street reeling around him. His last sight before the door was shut on him with a resounding thud was the child peering around the doorframe, sobbing with fright. He saw the birthmark and before the darkness claimed him, two words imprinted themselves in front of his eyes, written in the black, block capitals of a screaming headline. BABY SPAIN.

It had been the talk of the country. How many kitchens had Charlie Piper sat in, his samples spread out on the table, talking to housewives about the Baby Spain case? The baby who had simply disappeared. Into thin air. The papers had been full of it for weeks. How, asked enraged editors, was it possible for a complete stranger to walk into a hospital and make off with a child? For months Baby Spain had been the property of every gossip and crank. She had been spotted being taken on a ferry to the Mainland; she had been sold to an American couple who were childless; she had been kidnapped by an evangelist church which was desperate for recruits. Daily there had been a siege at the baby's home. Charlie remembered the father. Shady character, he had, thought, feckless-looking. Charlie knew the type. He had met their wives in a hundred parlours across the countryside. At Christmas and for the baby's birthday, the reporters went back to Mr Spain, Charlie recalled, and he repeated his pleas to whoever would listen: Please give us back our baby. But the years went by and everyone forgot about Baby Spain, including Charlie Piper. He presumed she was dead; she had been a sickly child. Someday a shallow grave would be found in a ditch or behind a hen house. The country was full of such secrets. If there had even been a picture of her, Charlie thought, her memory might have survived longer.

But she had only been a few weeks old. Her only distinguishing feature was that birthmark, like a tiny strawberry, they had said, on her chin.

He rang his friend in the Castle. Mullarney was a drinking companion, an unkempt man, his jackets like boleros on his vast torso, his shirt tails always trailing outside his pants. Moon-faced and silver-haired he was like a superannuated fat boy. But he had a good heart. Once or twice when Charlie had got into scrapes – after-hours drinking and the like – he had rung Mullarney who had put a word in for him. In return, he had kept his eyes and ears open. It was, Charlie considered, a professional relationship between two men of the world.

'Mullarney,' a voice barked in his ear.

'Con,' Charlie started, 'Piper here, Charlie.'

'Charlie, old son, how's she cutting?'

'Grand, grand.'

'Are you about?'

Charlie could hear Mullarney shifting the phone to his good ear.

'No, I'm north side.'

'Ah, pity,' Mullarney said.

'Listen, Con, there's something I want to talk to you about . . .' He hesitated, the strange excitement of the past few hours since his flash of insight on Jericho Street, turning now to a kind of dread. 'Confidentially,' he added to cover himself.

'Shoot . . . just hope it isn't the licensing laws again. I'm beginning to wear out my welcome in that department.'

'No, nothing like that,' Charlie said.

He was very nervous now. The consequences of his dangerous knowledge were only beginning to dawn on him. He was breaking one of the unspoken rules of Granitefield, grassing on a fellow inmate. And thinking of Granitefield he remembered with a pang what they used to say about the women patients, how sometimes the treatment meant that they couldn't have children. But his own tense alarm, his need to have the thing confirmed, or dismissed out of hand, was more urgent.

'Spit it out, Charlie, I haven't got all day,' Mullarney interjected. It was probably all in his head. The next time he and Mullarney met, he would be introduced to the lads as the joker who thought he had solved the Baby Spain kidnap single-handedly. This gave him courage – the prospect of being laughed at.

'Remember the Spain case,' he ventured.

'Yes?' Mullarney said doubtfully.

'Remember, the baby who was kidnapped?'

'Yes, Charlie, we're not likely to forget, are we?' Mullarney replied testily. 'Our biggest unsolved case.'

'Well,' Charlie said, his voice cracking as he lowered his voice to a whisper. 'I think I know where she is.'

'Speak up, Piper, line's terrible.' Mullarney's voice was fading away.

'I know where she is!' Charlie shouted.

He had not meant it to sound so emphatic. Afterwards he would speculate if the telephone connection had been better, it might never have come out as a certainty. There was an astonished silence at the other end. He heard the phone being dropped noisily on a desk, then a hubbub in the background with Mullarney's excited voice rising above it: 'Get the Super. Break in the Baby Spain case.'

Charlie Piper had saved very few mementos from his time in Granitefield. He was not nostalgic by nature and once the memories of the pain with its accompanying loss of invincibility, had slid away, he recalled with no small sense of pride the little triumphs over the system, the busy trading he had mastered and the illicit goods he had managed to smuggle inside. In its way it had been a life of terrifying simplicity. He had been like a war racketeer and the years in Granitefield were in retrospect like a long campaign in the trenches. The same rules applied. Pleasure when it came had to be grasped quickly; in the midst of danger and death it acquired a gritty edge. The creature comforts – drink, tobacco, sex – were all tradeable commodities and acquired a price. Even information was valuable. Charlie Piper had not only dealt in oranges and cigarettes, but also medical verdicts. He had made it his business to get to know Mrs Guthrie in the records office. A young war widow, she was ripe and gullible material for the brand of doomed idealism that Charlie Piper peddled. She believed his story about wanting to devote his life to finding a cure for TB. 'When I get out of here,' he would tell her, 'I'm going to take to the doctoring. If I could have a peep at some of the files here, just overnight, so I can study them. Get myself prepared . . .'

In time he had seen almost every patient's charts and X-rays. He did not offer information but if he was asked he saw no reason not to sell it. He had his ethics too. Like a fortune-teller, if he saw signs of the grim reaper, he did not divulge it. They would know soon enough, he reasoned. And the information was not all for gain. He chose Irene Rivers' file out of curiosity, and because she was no longer a patient, he kept the X-rays out after he returned her file to Mrs Guthrie. Even when he was stowing them away in one of his secret stashes he was not quite sure why he wanted them. They were, after all, only shiny black and white sheets which showed the world in reverse. What was light outside, was shade inside, the bones an eerie luminescence, while breath was rendered a dark, solid mass. He knew there was something lurid about his interest. He remembered the evening when she had stripped for him; it was as if she had been showing him this – he held the X-rays in his

84

hand – her cloudy and mysterious interior. He was looking for clues, he realised, something inside that would explain her to him. And when he left Granitefield, he could not bear to jettison them. He saw them as a good-luck charm, an illicit gift. And he felt absurdly grateful to her as if she had offered him her very soul. And now, he realised, too late, how he had betrayed her. Standing as he always had on the threshold of her life. Holding the hand of a child who could have been his. He felt like a spectre, a man cheated by a death that had not occurred. His own.

'That's the last we'll see of him,' Stanley declared, 'I showed him, didn't I, Pearl?'

Pearl nodded weakly.

Irene imagined the scene. Stanley, meek at first, then suddenly enraged, towering over a sprawling Charlie Piper, his arm raised weakly against Stanley's boot. Irene had seen this transformation before. Stanley might be slow to anger but once he was . . . But she saw how useless his aggression was in the midst of this intricate mess. But then, Stanley didn't know. How could he understand the enormity of his crime?

As soon as Stanley told her, Irene knew they were doomed. She felt the cold creep of implacable recognition of one who has come face-to-face with death. Stanley thought he had seen Charlie off. Irene knew better. She knew that Charlie would work it out somehow. He would do it out of pride and curiosity. He was used to being well-liked; he would genuinely want to know what he had done wrong. When he collected debts on the wards, Irene remembered, he would be perplexed if patients grumbled about coughing up (coughing up, Charlie would grin, get it?) He had made a deal with them, after all. He might not come back here for an explanation, Irene knew, but he would find it elsewhere. Her heart sinking, Irene considered the neat inevitability of it. Charlie Piper delivering her to her fate.

She readied herself for flight. From the attic she retrieved the suitcase she had brought from Granitefield. When she opened it, a cloud of dust billowed forth, releasing with it the pungent smell of must, sharp and green. Stealthily she packed for Pearl and herself; she had no plans, no idea where she would go, escape her only ambition. As she put Pearl to bed that night, she lingered longer than usual in the child's room. She remembered Stanley hanging the wallpaper, birdsong on a summer's night, the windows thrown open to dispel the smell of drying paint and paste. She gazed at the army of soft toys and rag dolls sitting in a row against the bed-head, a pillow of fur around Pearl's head. Her small shoes abandoned, pigeon-toed, on the mat, her dress splayed in a fan across the chair. She sat on the edge of the bed as Pearl snuggled into the crook of her arm, already drowsing. She read from *The Sleeping Beauty*, the longed-for child, the grateful parents, the wicked witch . . . but she stopped short of the handsome prince. Pearl was already asleep, mumbling softly, already leaving her for another world. Tomorrow, Irene would tell her. She would recount the days of stolen happiness, the picnics on the windswept hills, the seaside outings paddling in the shallows, the day she first walked, tottering down the street after Stanley as Irene let go of the reins, the trip to the Causeway, Stanley and Pearl picking shells on the head-land, the pride Irene had felt pushing the baby carriage out into the sun by the front door, her first words. She would have to know the dangers there had been too . . . the polio that had nearly crippled her, the day she nearly drowned . . . Whatever happened, Pearl must know these things. Her history. But it was too late tonight. Irene rose and kissed Pearl on the forehead, inhaling the tactile warmth of the child's skin and her milky smell, the soft shudder of her breathing already becoming a memory, a loss.

It was noon, a Sunday morning, the shocked stillness of the Sabbath. Three constables stood at the door of Number 24, Jericho Street. Taylor led the expedition, a lean man with sandy hair, troubled with scruples about the task at hand. Procedure and jurisdiction had determined that this arrest was his baby. He squared his shoulders and rapped the wood with his knuckles, a brisk tattoo. Its clatter reverberated on the deserted street. As they waited, he turned to his companions and said: 'Let's make this as civilised as possible.' But he feared the worst.

Stanley answered the door. He was in his stockinged feet, a stocky man in crisp white shirt and braces, still wrestling with his collar studs. His jaw dropped. This guy knows, Taylor thought, guilty as sin.

'Yes?'

'Mr Godwin?'

'Yes.'

'We'd like to have a word with you.'

Taylor edged his foot between the door and the jamb and gauged Stanley's weight and strength.

'It's about Mr Piper, I suppose,' Stanley said. The bastard is going to press charges, he thought, couldn't take his punishment like a man.

'Perhaps inside would be better?' Taylor ventured. He was thinking of himself. He didn't want a scene on the street.

'Anything you've got to say to me, you can say to me here,' Stanley said blocking the aperture of the door with a stout arm.

Taylor decided to change tack.

'Is Mrs Godwin at home?'

'This has nothing to do with her. It was a private matter between Mr Piper and me.'

'And your daughter, Mr Godwin?'

'What about my daughter? Now listen, here . . . ' He moved quickly to shut the door but Taylor, anticipating him, rushed at him, his two companions moving in behind.

'What the . . . ' Stanley gasped as the three strangers tussled with him in the hallway, pinioning him to the wall. Behind him at the foot of the stairs, a woman stood holding a small girl by the hand.

'Mrs Godwin?' Taylor asked, releasing his grip on Stanley's arm.

'That's right,' she said quietly.

'I think you know why we're here.'

'Yes,' she said simply. 'He knows nothing. I'm the woman you want.'

Taylor knelt on his hunkers and took Pearl's hand. Pearl frowned and looked up at Irene.

'This kind man is going to take you on a trip,' Irene said, her voice glittery, her eyes bright with tears, releasing her grip on Pearl's hand and prodding her gently towards the policeman.

'He's going to take you across the river, he's going to bring you home.'

Stanley watched blankly as Taylor led his daughter away. She went meekly, trusting Irene's bright tone and mistaking Stanley's incomprehension as compliance. From the street he could hear one of the constables saying to Pearl 'We're going in the car, would you like that?' and the beginnings of Pearl's whimpered protests as Taylor shut the door on them. He looked at Irene and saw a stranger. He had understood absolutely nothing. She turned her back on him and Taylor led her into the parlour. He was relieved that the operation had been achieved with a modicum of dignity. It was the last Stanley saw of his wife. The second constable ushered him out of his own home, the song of Solomon echoing in his head.

'*See, said the king, it is all. My child lives and thine is dead, on the one side, and Thy child is dead and mine lives on the other. Bring me a sword. So a sword was brought out before the king. Cut the living child in two, he said, and give half to one, half to the other. Whereupon, the true mother of the living child cried out, No my lord, give her the living child; never kill it! . . .*'

Taylor sat with Irene Godwin as the sun, tempered by sharp gusts, railed against the small house on Jericho Street, sank into a peach-coloured dusk. It was her only request – that she would be taken away under cover of darkness.

PART TWO

SHE WAS MRS MEL Spain. Who would have believed it? In the few months she had been married Rita struggled with the notion. She was in a constant state of amazement, bewildered as a dreamer who wakes to find the world has dispensed with all its jarring logic. She felt both omnipotent and helpless – all she had done was to *wish* for this. And yet, this life with Mel (*her* life she had to keep insisting to herself) still seemed outlandish. Every morning when she woke she would examine him lying there next to her. The thin menace of moustache, the clouded ridge of brow, the dark whorl of ear. She concentrated on these fragments in the hope that when she put them all together they would convince her. She watched his rituals avidly – how he smacked his face after shaving as if it were part of some rough penance, the vigorous grace with which he applied hair oil, the way he shrugged his shirt on as if he were a horse swatting flies from its flanks – in the hope that these might help her to believe. (His casual nakedness was still a shock, though. His pale haunch, a violet cargo of tongue and gizzard; she had not imagined it would be so ugly.) But so used was she to contemplating him from afar that she found this closeness rendered him unreal and mysterious. He remained the not quite attained dream, the distant object of longing, the youth with the shorn hair and cheery grin, the boy from the Mansions whom Rita *really* fancied. Like a birdwatcher, she had been satisfied with sightings. His figure emerging from a doorway, his hunched silhouette toiling up a rainy street. Even passing the dairy on Gloucester Street where bored gangs of boys lounged and smoked butts, was less of an ordeal if he were among them. Rita would suffer their sly, sidelong glances and the great guffaws of laughter in her wake just to get a glimpse of Mel Spain. As for Mel, if he knew he was being so intensely observed, he never pretended, greeting Rita with a hearty 'How'rya!'

It unnerved Mel to waken and find her, beached and blurred, scrutinising him, yet lost in a dreamy distance.

'Give over,' he would mutter, sour with sleep. 'Don't look at me like that.'

'Like what?' She was afraid he might detect her sense of disbelief.

'Like you could see through me.'

Mel Spain was twenty-two, an usher at the La Scala Cinema, vain as a trumpet player in his black uniform with the red piping. He stood in the foyer swinging a string of torn-off stubs, whistling and snapping his fingers as if a band had just struck up. It was a Saturday afternoon. Matinées at the La Scala were noisy, crowded affairs. Seats snapping in the artificial night, scuffling in the aisles and a furious scrabbling at ankle level. This accompanied by industrious chewing — toffees that left fingers and seats sticky, ice-pops, garish and gaspingly cold. Boys joined in on the on-screen battles, ducking, crouching, pointing fingers that were guns or puffing up their cheeks pretending to be bombs which exploded as a frothy burbling in their throats. The films were already old when they came to the La Scala. The prints were flawed. The huge blue skies of Westerns were flecked with what looked like the crushed bodies of insects. The soundtracks cracked and farted. The La Scala had once been a variety theatre and still wore its tatty, showy costume. Brown, flocked wall-paper, gilted boxes by the stage, swing doors with milky glass panels marked 'Parterre' and 'Balcony', a sweeping stairway in the foyer that flounced like a neglected belle. It hosted a cocktail of bad smells. Waves of disinfectant from the lavatories, stale cigarette smoke and the acrid smell of thwarted sex. Thwarted alright, Mel thought ruefully.

'That one has the hots for you,' Joey said, poking Mel in the ribs as Rita Golden passed them in the foyer. Joey Tate, heavy-set and dour-mouthed, was the senior usher at the La Scala who spoke always in asides. Older than Mel by a decade, he saw himself as Mel's mentor; he wanted to see him right. He was a betting man; he lived on the vicarious crumbs of other people's victories and disasters. He took equal pleasure in both. Rita Golden was with Imelda Harris, a tall girl with coppery hair and a green gaze. Even though they had only left the convent three weeks before, Imelda already seemed to Rita like a woman of the world. She had started her hairdressing apprentice-ship at Eileen's (late of New York) salon. Late of New York; it gave the poky shop on Great Brunswick Street an air of glamour and experience, as did its proprietor. Eileen, leathery-skinned and smoky-voiced, who called all of her customers 'honey'. The girls parted on the street outside, Rita to cross the bridge over the river back to Mecklen-burgh Street, Imelda to meet a date on the north side.

It was a June evening, the sun cooling on the cracked pavements. A mild sense of dissatisfaction had niggled at Mel since morning. After he clocked off, he knew that he and the boys would hang around the forecourt of the Mansions as they had done since they were twelve-year-olds, trading boasts and insults. Later, they might have a few pints, a game of darts or billiards, then on to a dance. He might get to walk a girl home; there would be some feverish groping in a doorway, a patch of flesh exposed as a consolation prize. He longed for a break from the pre-dictable mechanics of boyhood companionship and the hot, laboured struggles – but rarely compliance – of a Gladys or Noreen.

'Go on,' Joey hissed, 'dare ya!'

Rita Golden had barely registered with Mel, beyond a vision of a schoolgirl in tunic and tie cycling down Mecklenburgh Street, her fair hair afloat, the wings of her gaberdine coat flying. The notion that she might harbour some feelings for him had never occurred to Mel; he would never know that Rita Golden had nursed a furiously melancholy crush on him for several years. Flattered by Joey Tate's narrow-eyed appraisal of his chances, Mel looked at Rita more closely. She was a tiny creature (four feet ten inches in her stockinged feet, he was to learn), with a nest of honey-coloured hair which seemed to clamour around her pert, pretty little face. Her eyes were impossibly clear, a blameless, baby-blue. And so out of boredom, and to match Joey's gruff challenge, he followed her.

Afterwards he would remember every detail of that journey, considering it now like the condemned man's path to the gallows. Over the stagnant river and down the dusty quays, the golden light of late summer dipping behind the domes and spires, a pink hue in the west. Left through a maze of cobbled alleys; then a piece of open ground, a large rubble-strewn patch. The Court Hotel which smelled of soiled carpets and stale hot dinners. St Xavier's, set back from the street, only the gable porch visible, old confetti gathering at the kerb and the frocked figure of the sacristan spearing litter with a stick. The Lido Café. Mc Mahon's the butcher's, sawdust dragged out on the street, the word VICTUALLER set in brown and beige tiles below the window. Glimpse of the chopping block like the rump of a fossilised mammal and the sheen of the circular slicer. And there at the corner of Mecklenburgh Street, he caught up with her, and brazen as you like, as he told Joey later, he kissed a startled Rita Golden.

What he didn't say was that he felt she had compelled him. The power of her yearning – the sum of three years' infatuation – reached out and almost felled him. And Mel Spain, off-guard and seemingly invincible, surrendered. Only when he felt the hunger of that first embrace – for him, the showy flick of a card, find the lady – did Mel realise that Rita's ardour was more powerful than any lazy affection he might be able to muster.

Three weeks later he took her to a derelict house on Rutland Street. For Mel it was an end, a way to be free of her hypnotic wistfulness. The house was propped up by two wooden crutches, as if it had polio. It smelt inside of damp masonry and a febrile rot. Underfoot, earth and rust-coloured rubble. Thistles sprouted around the shattered windows, the sills were bearded with moss. It was forbidden territory. Haunted. When she was younger, Rita and her friends had dared one another to go in there alone in the dark. A woman was said to have been murdered there, done in with a hatchet. Now Rita was here, but with a man (Mel, being four years older), which made it safe. And lying down on his spread-out jacket, that too was safe. And being stroked, his fingers in the crook of her neck, a hand on her bare thigh where he'd pushed up her skirt, murmuring words that sounded both venomous and sacred. He gasped when he touched her, as if it wounded him. And then . . . and then, it stopped being safe. Wan light drained from a mauve sky. Above, the rafters gaped . . .

They were living over her father's shop on Mecklenburgh Street. Golden's Boots and Shoes. This only added to Rita's incredulity. She would wander through the house – the musty, brown, front parlour, rarely used since her mother's death, the small front bedroom she had slept in for years, the cramped back kitchen giving off on to the shop – touching familiar things to reassure herself that she

97

was on solid ground. The framed photographs on the sideboard, the grandfather clock on the return of the stairs, even the cups and saucers all remained resolutely, and infuriatingly, indifferent. She resented their stubbornness, their refusal to conspire in her transformation. It was hard for her, when she was alone like this, to believe that anything had changed. Only when she stood in front of the dressing table in her old room, and saw herself multiplied by three in the triptych mirror, did brute reality intrude. Then she would wistfully try to imagine herself back in the winter before. Back to a time when she had been Rita Golden. Plain and simple. A convent girl, the apple of her father's eye, a late and much-longed-for only child. But the singularity of it defeated her, particularly when she looked down at herself, huge and distended, bloated to the size of two, and felt the sudden lurch of a baby's kick. The morning sickness, her sudden aversion to the smell of shoe leather, even the heaviness of pregnancy had not damp-ened her euphoria. But the violent struggle she could feel within as if this being was resisting *her*, terrified Rita; it punctured the sickening kind of dreaminess she had nursed from the moment she had first laid eyes on Mel Spain.

If Rita could not grasp the sudden tumescence of her new life, then Mel felt his world to be shrinking. At night from the front room on Mecklenburgh Street he could see the prow of the Mansions and he felt like a man stranded, an emigrant who has disembarked at the wrong port. He had wanted to get away. But the teeming world of the Man-sions, the noisy balconies and stairways echoing with bawl-ing rows and bawdy endearments, the ragged laundry hangdog on the communal lines, the battered playground, seemed huge and certain as an ocean-going liner, while he was becalmed, bobbing uselessly on a lifeboat with a fretful child-bride and a baby on the way.

A TINKER WOMAN had come to the door when Rita was six months gone. She heard the finger on the bell and waited, as she always did, for the hand outside to release the second chime. Once she would have bounded to answer. She always expected an extraordinary stranger at the door – a man, of course – a lost blood relation from the States or the pools man with news of a good fortune. The sandalled Franciscan, bearded and bird-eyed, barefoot even in the depths of winter, who doled out holy pictures, the soot-faced chimney sweep, even the piano tuner, she welcomed extravagantly as lucky emissaries from the outside world. But pregnancy had made her listless, and the smells of the trading street, a mixture of fumes and fetid fruit, left her queasy. She opened the door gingerly. A stout, weather-beaten woman stood outside with a sleeping child swaddled in a tartan rug on her hip.

'A few coppers for the child, God bless you, ma'am.'

The woman hoicked the child further up on her hip and swayed dangerously.

'I'd do the pendulum for you,' she offered eyeing Rita's bump.

Rita believed in signs. They ruled her life. Never trust a man whose eyebrows meet in the middle; never put a new shoe on the table. She had had her palm read. And sure enough, a tall, dark stranger had entered her life. Mel Spain.

She invited the woman in. She boiled milk for the child and filled the grimy bottle his mother proferred. He fed

99

hungrily, making loud, sucking noises, while his mother swung Rita's wedding band on a length of thread over Rita's belly.

'It's a boy,' she declared, showing a mouthful of gold.

Rita, splay-legged, rejoiced. This, at least, might make Mel happy.

It had never struck Rita that it would be hard to *make* someone happy. She thought it would just happen. Tutored by the oiled romance of movies she had not counted on the knotty perplexities of intimacy. The grinding silences at mealtimes, the grim scrape of cutlery. Her father worrying at gristle between his teeth while Mel wolfed hungrily as if there was a danger the plate might be whipped away before he was finished. He mopped up the grease with wads of white bread which he tore into pieces before stuffing them into his mouth.

'Any more?' he would ask with his mouth full.

She was afraid of his appetite. No matter how much she cooked there never seemed to be enough; she felt accused, as if she were being a bad wife.

'Oliver asks for more,' her father would say slyly.

Rita would stand up decisively and start stacking. For the first time in her life Rita began to resent him. His wronged silences punctuated with deep sighs as if he couldn't bear the heaviness of his disappointment. He had been like this ever since she had told him about being in the family way (that was how she had said it; not 'having a baby', *that* seemed too terrifyingly concrete). She had expected anger; what she got was defeat. He had denied her the chance to rail against him, to justify her love for Mel.

'Well,' he simply said. 'I hope you're satisfied now.'

It was Lily Spain who had insisted on the marriage; in years to come Rita would hate her for this; she blamed all the messy intricacies of her life on that ill-fated shotgun wedding. She had set up an expectation of respectable happiness which would dog Rita to the end of her days.

'Never let it be said,' Lily had warned Walter Golden in the parlour upstairs 'that any son of mine shirked on his responsibilities.'

She had come around for a 'pow-wow', as Mel had put it. Then, Rita and Mel had been able to joke about it. Like children who had outwitted the adults, they had sat together in this very room, racked with stifled explosions of laughter while above them, Mel's mother huffed and puffed and Rita's father appeased. Rita remembered how their wicked delight had made them reckless; they had sneaked into the darkened shop and done it again on the polished floor, among the bargain bins and the footstools. It was rougher than the first time; it had felt like a contest, as if they were wrestling with one another to see who would win. He pinioned her to the ground, his hands manacling her arms, his unshaven jaw scalding her cheek. She found herself struggling, while willing him to finish, aware suddenly of the profanity of this coupling within earshot of her father. He planted a love bite on her breast. By morning there was a blossom of a bruise.

'Did I do that?' he had asked.

She had expected remorse. But he was proud. Proud that he had marked her.

Except that Walter Golden knew the La Scala existed, he would have suspected his new son-in-law of being a criminal. He kept the hours of one, lounging in bed until noon, leaving the house at dinner time and not returning until the early hours. Like a hotel guest, Mel came and went. Days would go by and Walter would not see him at all, or if he did it was only as a shambling, tousled apparition framed for a moment in the doorway en route from bedroom to bathroom. In the mornings Walter was forced to tiptoe about and whisper; the sanctity of Mel's sleep was observed reverently as if *he* was the man of the house. He did not know which angered him most – seeing Mel or not seeing him. His presence irritated Walter, his swagger, his brutal unconcern for the misfortune he had brought upon them. But his absence gave no respite either. Rita's condition was a constant reminder. Walter had known no good could come of this marriage but he had not raised a word of protest. The child could have been adopted and Rita could have made a fresh start. But, in truth, he had been afraid of opposing her. Love, or whatever the puppyish infatuation she felt for Mel, had changed her. It had given her command. He had seen the mettle of her certainty and was frightened of it. He knew he was no match for her. It was ridiculous, but Mel had made a woman of her.

The workings of women were as mysterious to Walter Golden as the innards of clocks. There were lots of cogs and wheels he didn't understand the use of but even the minutest of them had teeth. He remembered his late wife's passionate wilfulness, the sudden descent of a gloomy mood, the equally alarming outbursts of gaiety. He was an ageing man alone, a merchant, a strictly over-the-counter man. He lived by the tenets of modest, honest trade. Quiet and honourable, he was at sea when it came to the stormy wilfulness of emotions. What you see is what you get, he would tell the customers in the shop, a declaration as much about himself as the merchandise.

'The trouble with you Wally, me boy,' his brother, Bartley, had said at the wedding, 'is that if it were left to you, nobody would be good enough for your Rita.' He let out a beery guffaw, hot and stale. 'So it might as well be this young lad Spain as anyone else.'

His wife, Gracie, shushed him. 'Poor Connie would have been very proud,' she said gazing regretfully at Walter.

Poor Connie, Walter thought, poor Connie indeed. Rita's mother would be turning in her grave; three years before she had collapsed in the shop, a blood clot to the

heart. He marvelled at his sister-in-law's provocative in-
sincerity, a delicate balance of sympathy and venom. Her
intention was to wound – but politely. Long years in
trimmings had made her a woman who examined everything; the stuff of Rita's dress, the table settings, the
bridesmaid's bouquet; she had already calculated the cost
of the reception. She fingered the pillars on the tiered cake
and changed the subject.

'Are these edible?' she asked.

Rita Golden was lost. Her own name seemed strange to
her, like a faint tinselly echo, or a glittering promise
withdrawn. Rita Golden had no history. No sooner had
she taken flight, a shaky fledgeling on a short, tentative
foray from the nest, than she had been preyed upon. She
no longer knew herself, a married woman, a mother-to-
be. Rita Golden, or the notion of her, was fading away.
Rita felt a mournful kind of pity for this motherless girl,
roaming the summer streets full of a vague and tender
optimism. For a brief time Rita Golden had lived and then
she'd been killed off by getting what she had always
wanted. The boy from the Mansions.

THE BABY CAME early. Rita woke, paralysed by some instinct, and listened to the ticking of her own body. That was how she saw it now, as something separate and wilful, which, if she moved gingerly, would not cause her grief. She knew something was wrong, or rather she was aware of an imminence, a bracing alertness in her limbs. She felt them crouching, ready to leap. The knowledge her body had, which she did not, frightened her. She ascribed this extra sense she seemed to have gained to the baby. She imagined it as a wizened old creature, wise in the ways of the world, wiser than she was. She listened to the throb and gurgle as if she had turned to liquid and then, almost as soon as she had thought it, the waters broke in one big glop. The sudden gush made her feel as if she had lost all her substance. She expected her belly to shrivel up like a balloon while she, having abandoned her gravity, would drift away high into the corner of the room. She lay for a moment, revelling in this sensation of release, before alarm registered.

'Mel, Mel . . . !'

His face was buried in the pillow as if to shut out all trace of her. He complained about sleeping with her. She was too big, he muttered. He groaned and opened a sticky eye. 'It's the baby, Mel, it's coming . . . '

All she could remember was the pain of it. A sluggish, damp pain alternating with a searing clenching in her groin as if her body wanted to keep its prize. She felt herself at sea, rolling and heaving on crashing waves, her brow drenched, sweat dripping from the tips of her hair as she battled with ropes to keep her boat afloat. But it was too heavy for her. She could feel the swell of an angry tide tugging beneath her, dragging her down.

'Push, push,' the voices roared above the din of her pain.

But she was too weary. Her shoulders ached, her hands were slippery from clinging to the edge. She felt she was going to be split in two, she and the boat alike, sliced into two halves.

'It's in distress . . .' she heard them say.

The crew rushed forward, a practised jailer's arm on each of her limbs.

They were going to throw her overboard. Women and children first . . . they cut her open.

She caught a glimpse of a bloodied little bundle, raw angry skin, a bloated head with a sodden down of black hair. She struggled to rise but they pushed her down. Someone mopped her temple. It was deliciously cool. It made her head feel as if it was floating above her body, which was throbbing viciously below her somewhere, lost in the depths.

'Where's my baby,' she tried to say but as in a nightmare no voice came out.

'Hush there,' a nurse said kindly, 'it's all over now.'

'But . . .' She stretched out a hand, appealing, but found only thin air. There was a lot of movement suddenly, an urgent clamour, and she realised that it was she who was moving. Doors swung open and she was drifting through them. The boat was afloat again, the harbour in sight. She lay back, she surrendered.

As Mel Spain stepped out of the hospital – just for a walk, he told himself, a breath of fresh air – he was lighthearted for the first time in months. He felt as if he was leaving a great burden behind. The bustle of the labour ward reassured him. Its officialdom, the white coats, those capable nurses with their tiny watches pinned to their breasts relieved him. It was as if they were taking charge of all of his unwanted responsibilities. With a wave of the hand, they had seemed to absolve him. There was an end to this mess; *they* would take care of it.

It was chilly outside and beginning to rain. The lights of a pub across the street caught his eye. There was a golden gleam from its windows, the brasses on the door winked merrily at him. As he pushed his way through the crowd, the hearty sound of revelry cheered him. He felt he was rejoining the world. He sat by the bar and ordered a drink. All around him was a crush of bodies, a woman's clear laughter within earshot. In the mirrors behind the bar he could see his reflection, a lone, young man in the midst of a Friday night throng. At first he felt tempted to talk to the barman, to tell him he was about to become a father. But the longer he sat there the more buoyed up he felt by his own anonymity. There was no need in this company to admit who he was. Nobody knew him here and nobody cared. He could be a commercial traveller passing through the city, a sailor on shore leave. In his pocket he had a brown envelope with his wages for the week. He was out and he was free.

The obvious simplicity of escape astounded him. Ten years earlier, Alfie Spain, father of six, had left the Mansions one Sunday morning to buy a newspaper and had simply never come back. He wasn't even wearing a coat, a fact that Lily Spain clung to for years as proof that some tragedy had befallen him. Mel and his mother scoured the early morning dockers' pubs, the seamen's hostels and hunted among the down-and-outs squatting in doorways. He could have lost his memory, she said, and when that excuse wore out, she insisted that he must have been set upon by thieves.

On her insistence, the river was dragged. Every body that was washed up had to be viewed. By the age of twelve, Mel Spain had seen more corpses than an undertaker. It was only when he rebelled and refused to go to the city morgue to check out one more bloated or mangled body that his mother gave up the ghost. But she still set a place at the table for his father and for years she expected that he might just rove in one day, the paper under his oxter, as if he had just popped down to the newsagent's and been delayed. He had been a law-abiding man, a dutiful father, a loyal husband. He had shown no irritation at his circumstances, straitened though they may have been. They were always short, but Lily got by using cheap cuts and strict rations, and resorting to the pawn shop coming up to Christmas. Alfie Spain had left no debts. He was the kind of a man who handed over his wages every week to his wife, keeping back just enough for a few pints on a Saturday night which he drank quietly at the bar while Lily sang her head off and joined in the knees-up in the ladies' snug. Years later, a neighbour claimed he had spotted Alfie on the Mainland working on the roads. There were rumours that he had a second family over there but Lily put that down to bad-mouthing.

If the Spains were stretched before Alfie left, they were downright poor after he had gone. Mel's two elder brothers were put to work; Michael inherited his father's job on the docks, Peter was apprenticed to a printer. His sister, Bonnie, was taken out of school and sent to the shirt factory; Esther was dispatched to relations. Baby Martin – even as a grown man he was lumbered with this title – took on a paper round. Lily did charring and battled with the moneylender and in time, it seemed, that they didn't need Alfie Spain any longer, if they ever had.

It didn't stop Mel wondering, however, how his father had managed this extraordinary trick of disappearing into thin air. He had become invisible by simply walking out of his life. Ten years after the event, as he nursed his fourth drink of the night, Mel finally understood how easy it must have been. It was not, as he had always thought, a daring but calculated move; it was a matter of impulse and exquisite selfishness.

Mel staggered out of the pub at closing time. The seething wet streets greeted him, the sizzle of tyres. The street lights glimmered. He stood in a hazy blur, his resolve momentarily dissipated. The pillared rotunda of the hospital beckoned like a great belly. He turned his back on it. A fog horn bellowed in the night as he made his way up the quays. Flocks of seagulls swooped low over the river, cawing for rain. He passed huge, bleached warehouses and the belching urns of the brewery, the copper dome of a church; he felt himself walking into the silhouette of the city. The mail boat was already berthed, its great hulk yawning in the night. It would swallow him up. He felt invisible among the crowd of passengers gathered on the quay weighed down by suitcases and kitbags. Unlike them, he was shedding his old life, not carrying it with him.

Only the ghostly figure of his father accompanied him. He had only ever considered his father from the perspective of one left behind. He had become all absence, the vacant place at the table, the man who had never materialised as the nameless body in the morgue. There were times when Mel had longed for him to be dead, so as to rid himself of the anxious imminence his mother had cultivated in all of them. Now that he was here, literally following in his father's footsteps, Mel felt his father becoming a presence again, his pulse racing as Mel's was, his palms sweating, his glance darting here and there, fearful of being detected, as if the enormity of his intention were obvious from his features. He had already committed a crime by just being here.

'Mel!'

For a moment, Mel thought he had conjured up a ghost as if this was as far as his father had got, locked in a purgatory of being forever on the brink of departure, a man condemned to the quayside for having wanted to escape.

'Mel Spain!' the voice called again.

A gloved hand was clamped on his shoulder. He turned slowly, expecting to see an incarnation of his father, or a live policeman, and found Arthur Prunty. Captain Prunty was the manager of the La Scala, an ex-army man whose voice boomed as if he were still commanding parade drill, his exchanges like hearty attempts at boosting morale.

'Impossible to find anyone in this mêlée. I'm looking for the sister-in-law. Coming to stay with us for a spell.' He grimaced.

'Are you seeing someone off? One of the wife's people, is it? Any stir on the baby?'

Mel gulped. Every one of these questions was a trap.

'Ah, there she is!' He pointed to a frail, arthritic-looking woman perched on a suitcase and gripping two others on either side of her. 'How on earth did she think we'd find her here? Oh well, the mountain must come to Mohammed.'

'Bernie!' he shouted and grasping Mel's arm propelled him towards her.

'Give us a hand there, Mel; my god, would you look at the amount of luggage she has. All that for a few weeks!'

He handed Mel two of her bags while he unceremoniously heaved his sister-in-law up and swinging the last of her suitcases, he frogmarched her through the now thinning crowd, with Mel dejectedly following.

'I have the old jalopy outside,' he shouted to Mel over his shoulder, 'I can drop you off.'

Delia Prunty and her sister chattered in the back while Mel was ordered to sit up front with Captain Prunty. He treated the car gingerly as if it were new or delicate. It was like a black bathtub on wheels, Mel thought. Though he talked of it dismissively, Captain Prunty was inordinately proud of the car. He liked it to be admired, its patient gleam, its doughty engine. He wanted to be congratulated for it, in the same way as other men would appropriate compliments to their wives, or bask in the scholarly achievements of their sons. As Mel watched him wielding the crank handle he realised with a foolish sense of shock that he had allowed Captain Prunty to bundle him away, to bully him – albeit good-humouredly – out of his chance of escape. Was this how lives were turned, he wondered, on such small, banal choices? For him a careless kiss on the corner of Mecklenburgh Street in the boredom of a long summer's evening, and a chance encounter on a quayside with a man whom he had always considered to be a puffed-up old fool. The windscreen was clouding over with a fine rain. He made to wipe it, to clear a space through which he could see clearly, and realised that it was his own eyes that were misting. The drink, he told himself as Captain Prunty with one last yank of the handle set the engine throbbing.

MEL SPAIN was missing for three days. He crossed the river and booked into the Seamen's Hostel on the north side. The night had been misty; by the early hours of the morning it was a pea-souper, the perfect weather to disappear into. Foghorns groaned. Out there on the high seas – where he should have been – beneath the stroke and eclipse of the twin lighthouses which guarded the bay. He imagined his other self out there, living the life *he* should have had. A purser on a cruise ship, like the *Queen Bea*, or a musician in the lounge orchestra. A white uniform with golden epaulettes and squeaky shoes, the rich rustle of satin on the floor, the reek of cigars. The ocean lapping on the starboard side, a roving band of men for company who could speak several languages and could buy rum on the black market, a native girl in every port. Tropical music, the fruity pout of marimbas . . . A man groaned in the bed beside him. The dormitory stank of male sweat and musty blankets. The nights were punctuated by the snoring protests of dreams smuggled into the dark hours. He had missed the boat. Another foghorn moaned. Oh yes, Mel laughed sourly to himself, he had really missed the boat this time.

He slept the days away in a nest of soiled bedclothes, venturing out only at night to the dingy dockers' pubs down by the river where he wouldn't be recognised. He drank his wages away, stumbling back to the hostel in a blurred daze, falling into bed again, muttering in his sleep. He woke to the grey dawn of the third day, penniless, his mouth tasting of ashes, stubble on his chin. He looked down at his rumpled, sour-smelling clothes, his hair slicked flat, grazed his fingertips against the roughness of his chin and came to his senses. What was he doing out here when his son needed him? (Mel never had any doubts on that score.) Vanity prevailed. He would have to go home, clean up, get washed and shaved, put on his Sunday best and order flowers for the mother of his son.

Two hours later, the proud father arrived at Rita's side, bouquet in hand, with a great welcome for himself. He had announced her name at reception with a proprietorial air – my wife, he could hear himself boom, Mrs Spain. And the porter had replied, with equal respect, Mel thought – this way, Sir! He had stopped at the nursery on his way up but he could see no lusty specimen who could possibly be his, so he marched with as much purpose as he could muster for a man trying to hide his foolishness at carrying flowers. Rita was sleeping and he stood over her just watching for several minutes, the glow of paternity extending even to her, his child-bride. From behind his ridiculous blossoms he reached out tentatively to touch her fingers. Her eyes snapped open.

'You bastard,' she hissed.

Rita would have been surprised if she knew how Mel had spent his lost days. The last she saw of him was in the waiting room, his collar turned up, rattling small change nervously in his pocket. She suspected, of course, that he had been off with another girl. One of the usherettes at the La Scala, the small one, she thought, with the peroxide hair and the ladders in her stockings. She was amazed at how calmly she could consider a prospect which days ago she would have thought catastrophic. In the days since the

birth she had been prone to sudden tears – over the puckered gash on her stomach and the empty cradle at the end
of her bed. But her errant husband – she still had difficulty
with the word – induced only a hard-headed spite. It did
not much matter where he had been or who he'd been
with; the fact was that he had abandoned her in her hour of
need. Though still groggy – the room swung if she closed
her eyes – she had never seen things so clearly. It was as if
she had blinked and the world had exploded briefly like
fireworks in the night sky, and she was now witnessing
their fall to earth in a thousand false, glittery pieces. She had
imagined that having a baby would have made her lighter;
instead she felt anchored, weighed down by the facts of her
life – she was eighteen, a mother of a baby who had been
cut from her and taken away as if she were not a fit person,
and married to a man – no, she amended, a boy – who
profferred his ridiculous blossoms and beamed at her as if
nothing had happened. As if nothing had changed.

'It's too late,' she said turning away from him.

'But I'm here now.'

'It's too late,' she repeated.

He felt something slipping from his grasp – his life, the
only one he had.

Everything about the baby alarmed Mel. A girl, her small-
ness, the birthmark. An angry strawberry pucker on her
chin.

'What's that?' he had asked his mother who brought him
down to the nursery to show him his daughter. What he
saw was a ragged-clawed little monster in a cage, the blue
tributaries of veins and arteries like a relief map drawn on
her skin, her fontanelle beating, furious and delicate.

'Oh that,' she said disparagingly.

Nothing about birth – or death – surprised Lily Spain.

'That'll disappear . . . in time.'

Later she would come to rue these words.

THERE WAS a hex on her, Rita believed. She blamed the tinkers. She remembered the woman who had called to the door at Mecklenburgh Street, the one who had divined that the baby was a boy. Once Rita had crossed the woman's palm with silver she believed that she had entered unknowingly into some kind of demonic bargain. The spinning gold token held over her had been enough to cast the spell of ill luck. The tinkers had a claim on her child; she would never properly be Rita's. She remembered, too, visiting the market on Great Britain Street with Mel. Every Saturday the tinkers set up along the crumbling pavements. Mountains of clothes, tangled limbs of scarlet and silver sat in the gutters. Women scavenged through the spangled mounds, drawing out slivers of green and ropes of white. The toothed cogs of machines, sprockets and hinges, washers and nails were piled on upturned boxes. Bits of engines sat on the cracked kerbstones, rust-coloured spare parts, the jaws of implements. Everything for sale looked unfinished as if it had been torn from something else. Mel loved the market. He was a hoarder by nature. Perhaps from the La Scala, he had picked up the habit of always looking at the ground. You wouldn't believe, he would tell Rita, the things people leave behind them in the cinema. He pocketed what he found – umbrellas, hat-pins, single gloves, stray coins, and occasionally, a fat wallet.

Rita, big with child, loitered by his side as he rummaged through greasy nuts and bolts, the strewn innards of clocks.

This, Rita reasoned, must have been how the tinkers kept tabs on the baby she was carrying. Once, she was sure, she had spied the bruised woman who had come to the door. She was certain she recognised the threadbare shawl, the gold glint of her smile.

Every morning as Rita padded painfully down to the nursery she thought of that woman, recalling what she saw now as the knowingness of her smile. Slack-bellied, scarred, her baby wrenched from her – all of these things seemed like bad omens. There was nothing she could do but watch helplessly as the little creature (Rita couldn't even think of this stick-like being as a baby) laboured and struggled behind glass, a tiny blur of flesh. Rita could not bear to hear the horrible enlargement of her breathing, or to see her sprawled, frog-like, in the incubator, her tiny, claw-like fingers gnarled in her mouth. She watched, horrified, as the nurses slid her out from the glass tent to feed her and how she recoiled from the awful touch of another skin. Rita refused to hold her. The baby was too weak. Just looking at her hurt Rita. As if a look from her might kill.

'Don't you worry, Rita,' Dr Munroe said clapping a hearty hand on her shoulder, 'she'll be as right as rain in a few weeks.' He stood beside her as if surveying his handiwork. 'I've seen smaller scraps than this turn into great big hefty brutes. You'll soon be back complaining that she's eating you out of house and home! Isn't that right, Mr Golden?' He chuckled to himself as he walked away.

'There, you see, Rita.' Her father stood rubbing her arm appeasingly. Rita suspected he liked the feel of the dimpled stuff of her dressing gown.

But she wasn't comforted, not by him. Since the baby he had been tiptoeing around her as if she might turn nasty on him. He was ascribing some power to her that she did not have, but she did not have the energy to tackle him. Instead she let him lead her gingerly back to the ward.

Mel's mother was there admiring the eight-pound baby boy the woman in the next bed had borne. There was no respite here, Rita thought; it was a choice between viewing her own failed attempt or being surrounded by the squealing successes of others.

'Aren't you a little cutie,' Lily Spain was cooing, nuzzling her lips close to the baby's forehead. 'Wouldn't you just run away with him?' Nobody, Rita thought sourly, was going to run away with hers.

Lily hurriedly returned the baby to his crib at the end of the next bed. She settled herself down as Rita clambered painfully into bed. She was blissfully unaware of the underground resentment that accompanied her visits. No one had told her that Mel had abandoned ship for three days. For Walter it was no surprise; he treated Mel's disappearance as only to be expected, while Rita had been too ashamed to admit the fact that Mel had left her. But both of them, separately, wanted to punish Lily Spain for her son's fecklessness. Her very unknowingness seemed to provoke them.

'Has your milk come in?' Lily asked urgently.

Rita nodded miserably, aware of the hard globes of her breasts and the great brown saucers that were her nipples.

'You'll hardly have enough milk,' Lily went on, 'not with those little titties.'

Walter blushed and looked away. Titties; she used words like that.

Rita dreaded visitors. Aunt Gracie, Uncle Bartley, Mrs Spearman. They bounced into the ward bearing flowers or gifts for the baby, only to stop short at the empty crib. It made Rita feel like a fraud, as if she were a child feigning illness who had been caught out. To prove otherwise she would show anyone who would look the long scar on her stomach; she had counted the number of stitches. Imelda squawked and covered her eyes.

'Where's the baby, that's what I want to see,' Imelda said. But Rita would not willingly show the baby to anyone. She wanted her to look better. She did not want others to see her as Rita did, as something not quite human.

'Go on,' Imelda insisted. '*Please*, Rita.'

'I'm tired . . . it hurts to walk.'

'Well, then, I'll go down myself.'

She tripped out of the ward. Rita could hear her heels tapping down the corridor to the nursery. Then silence. She half-expected to hear Imelda scream or to be so shocked at what she saw that she would flee. She knew what a bad liar Imelda was. If there was trouble at school, Rita remembered, the nuns would always ask Imelda who was responsible. She would stammer, and instantly incriminate herself or somebody else with her ham-fisted attempts at deception. She couldn't even take a prompt, Rita remembered. She would blush and stumble when reading aloud, while all around her the air hissed with the word she was reaching for. She pored over her blotched copybooks magnifying her mistakes. It had made Rita feel good to know that Imelda would always be worse than her. Now as she sat waiting for Imelda's verdict, Rita remembered how she had exulted in telling Imelda she was going to marry Mel. She had always suspected that this was the one department where Imelda might have a head start.

'He's such a dish,' Imelda had said eyes popping in amazement.

She would hardly be able to manage the same enthusiasm this time around.

She heard Imelda's footsteps return.

'She's a sweetheart, that lovely mop of dark hair and those squinchy little eyes. And her skin . . . the nurse let me touch her. Oh . . . Rita.' Imelda sighed.

It was Rita's turn to be chastened. She felt a rush of gratitude for her friend's generosity, followed by a dart of competitive envy. If Imelda could see these things in her daughter – her daughter, how strange it sounded – then why couldn't she?

'And such a little fighter . . . ' Imelda was saying. 'You should be proud of her. What are you going to call her?'

'John Francis,' Rita said sulkily. She and Mel had never even discussed girls' names.

'Oh Rita, you're a howl! Seriously though, what are you going to call her? She looks so pathetic down there with just Baby Spain on her name tag. Poor wee mite.'

Rita shrugged. 'Mary, I suppose.'

Even *that* had been decided for her. As she was being wheeled away, Rita remembered a nurse's voice close to her, pressing upon her some urgent question. In her fever she believed that she was dying and that this was the act of contrition being whispered in her ear. And so she started to pray druggedly 'Hail Mary . . . ' As it happened it was not she but the baby who was in mortal danger and the nurses wanted to baptise her quickly just in case. What they were asking was the name she had chosen; what they heard was Hazel Mary. Rita had said nothing of this to Mel. Why should she tell him anything? But she knew he'd have a fit over the Hazel bit.

'Mary?' Imelda queried. 'Just Mary, plain Mary? Is that because it was a virgin birth? I mean, it was your first time, wasn't it?' Imelda cackled. Rising, she bent over and kissed Rita on the temple as if she was as endearing as her baby. Rita caught the intoxicating whiff of perfume.

'Must dash. I'm going out on the town tonight.'

Rita felt frumpy and inert, her hair falling lankly around her face and a sour smell of baby coming off her. It must be the milk, she thought.

'What do you think of this colour?' Imelda asked flashing her fingernails.

'I did them at work today between clients. They called it pearly pink. Looks more like faded knickers to me.'

She laughed merrily and with a swing of her crimson coat and the clack of her black pumps, she was gone.

A WEEK LATER, Rita was sent home, leaving the baby behind. She was relieved. The hospital exhausted her. The round of visitors, the dispiriting trips to the nursery, the broken sleep. She was constantly woken by the hungry cries of babies and the sound of suckling. Their greed appalled her, the way they clamped on to the breast, the ferocity of their sucking. It looked to Rita like an assault, yet when she had observed the mothers around her feeding (what else had she to do?) she couldn't help noticing the dreamy calm they seemed to fall into when their babies were on the breast. It was a hypnotic kind of union, like being in love. She couldn't understand it; it both baffled and irritated her, this love-sickness.

Her father came to collect her. He stood sentry outside the drawn curtains as she dressed and packed her things. How little had really changed, she thought. She had been in hospital once before – to have her tonsils out and he had nursed her afterwards, feeding her tentatively with soup and ice-cream, and inept concoctions from the kitchen. If she closed her eyes she could just about imagine herself as a sick little girl and her daddy waiting to take her home. But she could only go so far with this fantasy; after all, what was wrong with her now even Daddy couldn't make better.

'Three weeks and she'll be all yours,' Dr Munroe said as she and her father gazed for the last time through the nursery window. 'And you can come every day to see her!' He beamed at them. Three weeks, Rita thought, a reprieve. She refused to consider the lifetime after that.

The house seemed to have grown strange. Dim and quiet after the din of the hospital, its rooms looked secretive and neglected and refused to grant her the gift of familiarity. The staircase was narrower and more forbidding than she remembered; the kitchen seemed to be sulking. It was a shock to find Mel there. The upheaval of the last week had convinced her that in her absence her past was being carefully pieced together again and that Mel, the wedding, the baby, were part of some nightmarish aberration, the product of feverish illness. But no, there he was, large as life, sitting in the kitchen, his mouth bulging with a half-eaten sandwich. Around him on the table were several opened jars of pickle and jam, a half-empty milk bottle, the splayed remains of a sliced pan. He looked guilty as if he'd been found with his hand in the till.

'Ah, Mel,' her father interjected. 'There you are.'

Rita recognised the forced heartiness of the tone, the one he might have used if he had come across the plumber on his hands and knees under the kitchen sink. It made her sorry for Mel, despite herself.

'Hello there,' he said, rising and pulling back a chair for her. She was oddly touched by the gesture; Mel had never been what she would have called a gentleman. She sat down next to him while her father busied himself noisily with the kettle. She found herself suddenly shy of him, afraid to meet his gaze.

Mel, sensing the air of truce, hazarded a smile and Rita, glad of being rescued, laughed ruefully. Her life with Mel would always be like this. A series of starting overs. Short joys, long penances.

For three weeks she became Rita Golden again. She squandered hours at Eileen's salon on Great Brunswick Street. It was close to the hospital so after Rita had dropped in to view her baby through the glass – she could see no change though the nurses purred about weight gain – she would call into the salon. If Imelda wasn't doing washes, they would sit in the curtained-off area at the back where the hair-driers were and chatter, or leaf through the tattered magazines, choosing styles for themselves. Imelda did Rita's nails, chiselling and scraping, then polishing her cuticles before applying varnish. It required her to be utterly still as Imelda held her hand and painted laboriously, her tongue inching out between her lips in deep concentration. At school they used to laugh at Imelda for this. Mother Alphonsus would say tartly – we don't use our tongues to write, isn't that right, girls! Now, Rita was glad of such uncomplicated attention. She was vain about her hands; they deserved to be pampered, they, at least, had remained unchanged. The rest of her body had been curiously altered. It did not feel her own any more. Throughout her pregnancy it had been clenched tight, now it sagged. Inside it felt slack and laggardly, dejected at having lost its prize so reluctantly borne.

One afternoon, when Eileen was out, Imelda offered to 'make her over'. Rita watched as she saw herself disappear under layers of powder and blusher, eyeliner and lip gloss. She felt, literally, like a new woman.

'Why don't we cut your hair?' Imelda asked as she stood behind her, lifting, then letting fall, her lank strands. Since the baby, it too had seemed colourless and dull.

'Why not?' she said taking up Imelda's tone of defiance.

Imelda set to. Rita saw the clippings spread at her feet in a carpet of fair down. It looked like baby's hair, curling and defenceless. She was glad to be rid of it. Instead of a dull weight around her shoulders, it bobbed cheekily at her ears. Rita was pleased with the effect. It made her look older, like a married woman. She emerged on to the street on a cloud of chemical whiff. She touched her hair as she walked; it felt tacky and stiff. She caught glances of herself in shop windows; she saw a taller, more stately reflection than she was used to. The perm gave her a couple of inches and made her feel like an African woman bearing something precious on her head. The packed foundation on her face was like an armour, a way of fending people off and her new hair-do, a helmet. She was delighted when she passed Mrs Spearman on Mecklenburgh Street who looked at her quizzically but couldn't place her.

'My god,' Mel said, 'what have you done to yourself? What's that muck on your face?'

He was standing in front of the mirror in the kitchen adjusting his bow tie, making ready to go out to work. She thought he would have been pleased. A glamorous wife as trade for a dowdy girl. Before she could answer, her father emerged from the shop.

'Have you told her?'

He didn't even notice her shorn locks.

'The hospital rang,' her father said accusingly.

'So?' She could hear the truculence in her voice.

'We can take the baby home.'

The triumph of his tone toppled her newly acquired sense of grandeur. She trailed up to the bathroom and scrubbed her face until it stung.

There was a carnival air as they rose the next morning. Mel and her father set up the spare room. The Moses basket, which had been Rita's when she was a baby, stood proudly in the middle of the room. Rita had made it up the night before, running her fingers along the soft winceyette sheets and the satin-rimmed blanket which Aunt Gracie had crocheted. Two towers of nappies sat on the bed beside a basket crammed with cartons of talc, cards of safety pins, a cloud of cotton wool, jars of antiseptic cream, a tiny nail scissors. Rita was amazed at how many accoutrements babies needed, little vain accessories to primp and pretty, as if they were greeting the arrival of a pomaded princess. She remembered buying these things but it seemed so long ago now, belonging to a time when the baby had been all possibility and enhancement. She plucked out the lace christening robe in which she had been baptised from the bottom drawer of the chest in her father's room – her mother had kept it for just such an occasion – and a pink matinée jacket which Lily had given her. The choice of these items gave her a sense of history and celebration; it convinced her that everything, finally, would be alright. She was being given a second chance.

Dr Munroe greeted them in the entrance hall of the hospital. It was a perfect round. Grim marble busts sat on pedestals in the alcoves under the long, high windows, filled with lozenges of the blue day. The tiled floor, radiating in a chequered mosaic at their feet, still bore damp patches and there was a faint smell of pine, adding to the air of newly scrubbed morning. Rita was anxious to see the baby. In her mind, her child had grown fat and bonny, ruddy-cheeked with dimpled arms, a baby a mother would be proud to claim. Rita was seized by a kind of excitement, her baby about to be delivered to her. She could safely wipe out the memories of the past few weeks now – the awful birth and the mechanised limbo to which her baby had been consigned. Now, with her husband at her side, her new life – *their* new life was about to begin. The loving mother, the proud father, the doting grand-father, she saw the three of them as a blessed tableau. A Holy Trinity.

'Mr Golden,' Dr Munroe said, smiling tensely. 'Can I have a word?' He drew Rita's father a couple of paces away.

There was some anxious whispering. She nudged Mel.

'There's something wrong,' she said.

'Don't be silly,' he said, 'everything's fine.'

She abdicated for a moment to his certainty, as she had done once before, holding fast to the picture of the holy family, even as her father approached.

'Rita,' he said quietly.

She stared at him. Something *was* wrong.

'Rita,' he said again, sharply, as if she wasn't paying enough attention.

'What, what is it?'

'It's the baby . . . she's gone.'

'Gone, what do you mean gone. Dead?'

An image of the baby trapped in her glass bowl passed in front of her. And then she indulged the notion of the baby not being in this picture. It was not wholly unpleasant, this wicked thought. The past months miraculously un-ravelled, the clock wound back, their coupling undone, her life before, intact. But it wouldn't hold, this vision of the past. Too much had happened. Too much.

'Somebody's taken her.'

Why is he talking in riddles, she wondered. If the baby is dead, why doesn't he say so?

'Taken her. What do you mean, *taken* her?'

Her voice came out as a shriek. Its shrill echo rebounded back at her in the colonnaded hallway. Dr Munroe stepped forward.

'I'm so sorry, Mrs Spain,' he said, grasping her at the wrist and elbow as if to restrain her. (Some kind of status was being conferred on her after the event. Dr Munroe had always called her Rita.)

'Nurse Matthews left the nursery for two minutes after the feed. Just two minutes,' he insisted contritely, appeal-ing directly to her father. He refused to meet her gaze. 'Such a thing has never happened before. Some woman, they say.'

He wrung his hands absently.

'Some desperate woman.'

She should never have let them take the baby away from her. That was her first mistake. No, she corrected herself, she should never have let that tinker woman touch her; *that* was her first mistake. They had come, as she knew they would, they had come and stolen her baby from her. If she had only held the baby, just once, maybe *that* would have broken the spell and unhinged the hold they had over her. Or if she had fed her from her own breast? If the baby hadn't been incarcerated in that tent. She should never have allowed that. No, no, she argued with herself, it went back further than that . . . But no matter how far back Rita went, she could not gainsay the terrible truth; that someone had wanted her baby more than she had.

FOR WEEKS Golden's Boots and Shoes on Mecklenburgh Street was besieged. Neighbours crowded into the back kitchen where Rita sat, surrounded by small mounds of baby clothes which she sorted absentmindedly by colour and by type. They brought food; it was all they could think of doing. They had never eaten so well, Mel thought. Trays of sandwiches appeared from nowhere, a pot of stew bubbled on the stove. Blancmanges, trifles, bowls of jelly sat about the place unheeded. These were for Rita – to tempt her to eat, as if she were a picky child who had to be coaxed. Pots of tea were on the go all day. Damp tea towels sat on every chair. It was, he thought, like the aftermath of a wake, except there had been no death. A knock would come to the hall door and Mel would answer it. There would be a reporter slouched against the jamb.

'Any news of Baby Spain?' A query accompanied by a chromium flash.

Mel found himself elected as the family spokesman. He got used to the click and whirr of cameras, the endless queries roared at him from the street.

'Are you happy with the police investigation, Mr Spain?'

'How is your wife bearing up, Mr Spain?'

'Have you anything to say to the kidnapper?'

Mel found he had a gift for it, this loud, indelicate camaraderie. And it was *his* face which appeared on the front pages of the newspapers under declamatory head-lines: HEARTFELT PLEA BY FATHER OF SNATCH BABY; BABY

SPAIN NEEDS HER MOTHER, SAYS KIDNAP DAD. He liked the image it gave of him. The reporters ascribed to him words and statements that made him seem like a man of authority. He was suddenly at the centre of things, firm and capable, acting the part of the grieving father. In truth, he was not grieving. Mel believed at that stage that the loss of the baby was temporary, a brief suspension of normality. Some other mother had taken the wrong baby home, he told himself; after all, they all looked so much alike. He felt too much lazy goodwill about the world to believe that the taking of the baby was sinister or calculated. And he would never believe that she was dead. For years to come – even after Stella was born – he believed that one day his long lost son would return. (He thought of her still as John Francis.) He imagined opening the door one day to a fine young man, a sailor with a kit bag or in a soldier's uniform, who had been out adventuring in the world and had come back with tall tales to tell. In the meantime, he stood on the doorstep on Mecklenburgh Street and thought of Gary Cooper; he had seen enough of his movies to know how to simulate quiet dignity. And raising his hand, he could command silence from the assembled huddle of the press.

He kept the cuttings; he knew it was inappropriate and so he did it quietly, storing the newspapers in bundles under the stairs and when the spotlight faded, secretly clipping and filing all the stories in a shoebox. He hid it at the bottom of the wall of boxes of old stock which lined the hall in Mecklenburgh Street. He was keeping it for the baby, he told himself. And if he savoured some personal glory from having this illicit record, he justified it as proof that would be needed in the future, proof of his strength in a moment of great adversity.

Rita had become the baby in the tank. People drifted into view, large, blurred, indistinct. They spoke, but like gold-fish mouthing through glass, she heard no words. She felt as if she were under water, a silent, green world of grief. Soon, soon she would rise to the surface, escorted by a spray of tiny bubbles and break the calm, thrashing and gasping, her first breath a great, agonised howl . . .

When, after several weeks, the neighbours withdrew with their bowls and plates, the reporters went back empty-handed to their offices, and the plain clothes detectives retreated with their unanswered questions, Rita's torpor gave way to a dogged determination. *She* knew where to look for her baby. The tinkers had taken her. One of their own had died and they had replaced her with Hazel Mary. (Rita whispered the name to herself to keep the baby alive, as proof that she had indeed carried a child and given birth.) She scoured the streets. Every Saturday morning she would go back to the market on Great Britain Street, sure that she would find the woman whose palm she had crossed with silver. It was this woman who had her baby. Mel would reluctantly accompany her.

'She's not here, Rita,' he would say as they walked among the leavings, the tattered clothes, the battered pots. 'We're not going to find her here.'

He held her hand; her air of distraction had made him tender. He was in awe of her desperation; he envied the extravagant expression of her loss.

'Let's go home, now. You're only tormenting yourself.'

Sometimes she would acquiesce, wilting suddenly and allowing herself to be led away. But, more often, she would pull away from him and stride off on her own.

Once, on the way back from one of these expeditions, she spotted a tinker woman begging on the steps of St Xavier's. There was a baby swaddled in a blanket on her lap. Mel had to run to keep up with Rita who darted across the busy street and made for the woman. She scrutinised the woman's thick plait of hair, her leathery girth, her snaggle-toothed face, her ill-shod feet.

'Give me my baby,' Rita commanded.

'Ma'am?' The woman gaped at her, her eyes two brown pools of amazement.

'You took her from me, give her back.' She tugged at the tinker's shawl. The woman, grasping at her skirts, struggled to rise.

'Rita, please . . . ' Mel tried to drag her away but she struggled against him. She was all elbows and rage. The woman's grip on her child tightened.

'This is my first to live, ma'am,' she said quietly. 'This is my treasure.' And turning, she scuttled away, peering anxiously behind her as she ran in case she might be followed. All the fight went out of Rita. She sank on the steps, sitting supplicant, defeated, those words ringing in her ears. My first to live.

That was when she decided. Hazel Mary was dead. The story of the kidnap had been a game, a way to save her from fearing the worst, that her baby had been dead all along. The creature in the tent had been an impostor; no wonder she hadn't loved it. Hazel Mary, *her* Hazel Mary had died at the moment of birth. That was why they had whisked her away. Mel and her father and Dr Munroe had concocted the story about the kidnapping. All that talk about reporters at the door asking about ransoms and rewards had all been part of an elaborate fabrication. First, they would tell her the baby had been taken, then, when she had got used to the idea, they would tell her the truth. A truth she had already tumbled to.

She went back to the hospital. In fact, she haunted the place, where so recently she had dreaded going. She paced the corridors of the maternity ward, halting at this bed, and then another, eyeing their occupants, peering at their babies. She followed the nurses, badgering them to tell her what they had done with her baby. She singled out Nurse Matthews, who had been on duty that day; she would definitely know, Rita decided.

'I'm sorry, Mrs Spain. I'm *really* sorry. I was only gone for a few minutes. And she was doing so well, before . . .' She halted.

Rita heard the remorseful pause. Now, she willed her, now, tell me. She was doing so well before she died. But all Nurse Matthews said was: 'If I could bring her back, believe me, I would.'

Finally, Dr Munroe took her aside. He showed her into his office. On the walls were charts of the human skeleton, the red veins and blue arteries like the complicated depiction of a railway junction. Dr Munroe did not sit down. He loped back and forth as if he were a prisoner on designated exercise, his hands sunk deep into the pockets of his coat. He was working himself up to it, Rita thought, gauging his every movement.

'We think it would be better, Mrs Spain, if you stopped coming here,' he said, still pacing, his head sunk on his chest as if he were musing to himself. He stopped.

'I'm sure the police are doing all they can.' He ran a hand distractedly through his straw-coloured hair. He paused and leaned over her.

'You can be assured that your baby is being well cared for. Whoever has taken her means no harm to the child. Probably a mother who has lost a baby of her own.'

'Show me,' Rita said, rising suddenly from her seat.

'Show you what, Mrs Spain,' he replied evenly.

'Show me what you've done with her. She's here. I know she's here. She's dead and no one will tell me.'

'Mrs Spain, there is nothing I can show you. Your baby isn't here. Your baby is out there, somewhere. Somewhere else.'

A shallow grave, he thought grimly to himself.

She hunted through the bowels of the hospital. The basement was a series of large, empty rooms, reached by a clattery service lift. Along the dim corridors were grey metal lockers and large cages of laundry. There were tall, slim cylinders with gauges attached, their red needles registered at nought. She could hear the sound of an engine running somewhere outside. She pushed open a large metal door and found herself in a small, enclosed yard. At the far end of it was a shed. She ventured closer. From the doorway she could make out the figure of an overalled man labouring in the gloom. He opened a hatch in the darkness. A square of leaping flames shot up illuminating the dim interior. He dumped something into it, a bag containing something soft and pulpy. The fire flared at his shoulder. He stoked it with a shovel, then turned to lift another bag up. His face was blackened, his hair singed, his eyes like pale moons in his sooty face, beads of sweat glistening on his grimy brow. Rita could smell burning flesh. She screamed.

'What the . . . ?' he yelled closing the iron grid at his back. It clanged dully, eclipsing the roar of the flames.

Rita fled. She had found what she was looking for. A glimpse of hell.

RITA HAD SEEN the vengeful hand of God. He had sent her baby to the burning fires of hell right before her eyes. She was being punished. The sin of the mother had been visited upon the child. She had thought that when she had said 'I do' at the altar in St Xavier's six months before that she had escaped his wrath. She remembered the pea-green light in the church and the soaring figures of the Trinity emblazoned in the stained-glass window in the nave. Father, Son and Holy Ghost. The eye of God in the glass had looked down on her that day and had seemed forgiving. But it had only been a trick of the light. His eye was so high up she had had to crane her neck to see; it was, she saw now, black and solid, lofty and cruel. She studied that eye many times, gazing fixedly at it. He had but one, one all-seeing eye; the other was eclipsed by the shadow of what Rita thought was an eyelid. She came to see it as a malicious wink. What she didn't know was that there was a hole in the window of the nave. Years before, a boy from the Mansions had climbed a tree outside the church and once he had reached the height of God's shoulder he had used his catapult to fire a small stone through the glass. He aimed for the bull's eye. It had gone clean through; he had taken out the eye of God. That boy was Mel Spain.

Rita spent many hours in the church amidst the hissing sibilance of solitary prayer. She knelt in the front pew within earshot of the drone of absolution from the confessionals and waited for a sign. It was not devotion which brought her there. No amount of prayer, she knew, could save a soul from hell. Indulgences could win an unbaptised baby from limbo or the throngs of pagans who had never known the face of God, but hell, hell was final and absolute. She was turning to God or was it the devil – she remembered the custodian of the flames at the hospital – in a desperate attempt to ward off worse. She made a bargain. He could take Mel, she offered, eyeing the lofty nave, he could even take Mel, if she could have her baby back.

Mel watched bleakly as Rita's hysteria turned to penitential resolve. It had been one of her saving graces that she was not a religious girl. In fact, he would never have got his way with her if she had been. At some stage in the tussle she would have called a halt, reclipped her rolled down stockings, tucked in her crumpled blouse and with a hand through her messed hair she would have got up and stumbled away. Mel had not believed his luck when she had not resisted. He remembered the intoxication of schoolgirl flesh, and Rita's ardent but tremulous submission. He ruminated nostalgically on these things in the months after the baby was taken. He had plenty of opportunity. It wasn't that Rita wouldn't let him touch her. He got plenty of hard little kisses. In bed at night, she would stroke the hair at his temples and croon at him endearments she had never used before: 'My pet', 'Pet lamb'. Pet lamb indeed. That's exactly what he felt like. Something soft and woolly that could be babied. But if he tried to hold her, lodge his tongue inside her mouth, she would wriggle free saying 'No Mel, not yet!' He did not know that she was practising for a time when he would be taken away from her.

He had reckoned on a period of mourning, three months he estimated at the outside. But as time passed and

Rita's scruples became more, not less pronounced, it began to dawn on Mel that perhaps this wouldn't pass. He would climb in next to her after a late show at the La Scala and find her curled like a warm, downy baby in the hollow of the bed, nightdressed to the neck. He would knead the skin he could only imagine beneath the rubbed cotton she wore, seeking out the curve of breast or hip, smuggling touches that now seemed forbidden to him. But his urgency would always give him away (he wanted to take her not to finger her) and she would wake finding his hand trying to worm its way in between her legs. He always took it away smartly as if he had been caught grave-robbing, as if his desire was unseemly. But she was his wife, after all.

He sought consolation in the dingy vulgarity of the La Scala and bouts of hot, furtive sex in the projection room with Greta, one of the usherettes. Romantic hostilities broke out between them from time to time; he never knew when he was going to get the go-ahead. Her indifference excited him. Weeks would pass and she would barely glance at him, sashaying about in her stained bri-nylon sweaters and too tight skirts, cradling her torch idly in her lap. She had a fringe and long black hair – out of a bottle, Mel suspected – and a dishevelled kind of glamour. She was older than him by several years; pushing thirty, the other girls said. He would feign disinterest too but felt he was less successful at it. He had the feeling that she knew what she was doing, whereas he felt the victim of her whims. After weeks when they would barely have exchanged a word, she would smile at him, all teasing invitation, and he would know that it was on. Her hunger outdid his own; there were times with Greta when he felt he was being devoured. She would suck and scratch and bray; sometimes he would have to clasp his hand over her mouth in case they would be heard above the rumble and boom of other love stories which shimmered bluely over their heads. Afterwards he would feel that he had been in a scuffle with someone, the fright of it still pounding in his veins mixed with relief that he had had another lucky escape. Never again, he would vow, but there always was another time. Until Greta left. Inexplicably. Captain Prunty said it was for personal reasons, a bereavement of some kind. The girls said otherwise. Mel pumped them slyly for information.

'Love life,' Celia Shortall said knowingly. 'Imagine, *she* had a love life!' Celia warmed to her subject. 'Someone broke her heart. That's what she said. Mind you, she was a bit tipsy at the time.'

'And who was it? Anyone we know.'

'Nah,' Celia said. 'Some married fella. I suppose when you get to her age that's all you can get.'

Mel was relieved. It was somebody else then, nothing to do with him.

The sacristan at St Xavier's was waiting for a miracle. In the dead hours of the afternoon he watched the young woman in the lace mantilla sitting in the front pew. Like most people on Mecklenburgh Street, he knew Rita's history, though with the passing of time the details became obscured so that the missing baby became reduced to some vague trouble of Rita's that she should be over now. Was she the girl whose baby was taken, they would muse, or was it a miscarriage? As he hurried about his business, the sacristan noted her stricken, imploring expression, the piety of her prayer. He would sneak glances at her, eager to witness the consuming light of beatification. She had the kind of face that might see visions. The gift came to those who were young; it was through them the Lord spoke. He polished the candlesticks, brassed up the altar rails, he bore in fresh flowers, readying his church (he regarded God as merely a joint owner) for a major spectacle.

Benediction came on an evening in December; the sky was a bowl of grey, the wind dank and chill. A sudden squall of rain had just started as Rita stepped into the church porch. She looked out at the greasy street and the spitting of the heavens, and felt the stirrings of defiance. It was two years now. Only the reporters kept the anniversary.

'Any news of Baby Spain?'

There would be some mumbling at the doorstep – they always asked for Mel – and they would leave dejectedly. Mel treated it as an inconvenience, a minor irritation as if he were being asked a technical question he didn't know the answer to.

Walter Golden would scowl and return to his accounts. 'Why don't they just let us be?'

Business was bad. After years of brooding calm, the city had erupted unble to contain its differences. Several bombs had exploded in power stations and factories along the river which marked the boundary between north and south. It made people wary and nervous of travelling into the city centre. And money was tight; his customers were saving their shoe leather.

There was an uneasy truce in the house on Mecklenburgh Street. Walter, Rita and Mel had the air of survivors, a small group with a shared ordeal in common. They never mentioned the baby. At the start it was incredulity that prevented them. There was no need since she would soon be back with them. It was only a matter of time. This deference had hardened over the years into superstition. Each of them buried her in their own way. Walter regarded the whole episode as an illness, as if Rita had suffered a breakdown or had been sent to a sanatorium. His memory of it was feverish, all blur and haze, a series of alarms and relapses.

Mel fuelled his rejection by blaming Rita. In some obscure way, he believed this was all her fault. She had trapped him with the threat of a baby, a baby that had vanished almost as soon as it had appeared, like a clever conjuring trick. Now you see it, now you don't. He did not wish to be reminded of how badly he'd been duped.

And Rita, Rita wanted it to be over. She hungered for and feared a final verdict. Any sense of imminence bothered her. A knock on the door, her name called out. She would watch anxiously as her father sliced envelopes open with his thumb and forefinger and drew out the letter inside. She could no longer answer the phone. Even the minutest silence before callers identified themselves made her quake. This, she would tell herself, this is it. Out on the street, the sound of scurrying footsteps behind her brought her to a shocked halt. She would turn around very slowly, bracing herself. A boy with a telegram. A man in uniform. In shops she expected to be paged, to be called away with news. But it was worst at home since either Mel or her father could judge at any moment that it was time to confirm what she already knew. That her baby was dead. She shook the rain from her scarf as she entered the church. Canon Power was reading from the lesson.

'*Pharoah's daughter came down to bathe in the river, while her maid-servants walked along the bank. She caught sight of the basket among the rushes, and sent one of her attendants to fetch it; and when she opened it, and saw the baby crying, her heart was touched . . .*'

The high altar was ablaze, a red carpet was rolled out in the aisle, there were garlands on the pews.

'*. . . Take this boy, Pharoah's daughter said, and nurse him for me; I will reward thee for it. So the woman took the boy and nursed him till he was grown; then she handed him over to Pharoah's daughter who adopted him as her son, and gave him the name of Moses, the Rescuer . . .*'

And lo, there were angels. They nestled in twos near the vaulted ceilings, cherubs with sculpted curls and tiny wings. One, stonily sightless, genuflected by the door beneath the weight of a scallop shell containing a low tide of gritty holy water. Another pair stood at each side of the altar on pedestals, one with a flaming sword, the other holding aloft the ruby glow of the sanctuary lamp. They wound into the bark of the pulpit; they trumpeted at the baptismal font, a well of grey stone. They trooped across the altar steps, small creatures gowned in red and white, marching down the aisle in formation towards her. A sweet, smoky, scent filled the air. A thurible chimed plangently. A golden sun was rising at their heads, its jagged, encrusted rays glittering. The litanies sang in in her head. *Mirror of Justice, Seat of Wisdom, Mystical Rose, Morning Star, Tower of Ivory, Mother of Christ, Mother of Divine Grace, Mother Most Pure, Mother of Pearl . . .*

As the procession passed before her, Rita inhaled its intoxicating smell and felt blessed and released.

SHE TOOK UP ballroom dancing. She went to Giuseppe Forte's Academy on Pitt Street. The studios (as Mr Forte described his tatty rooms above a draper's shop) were a large, neglected premises. Paint peeled off the walls, the stairs hosted a faint smell of mouse droppings, the lavatories stank of rot. But when Mr Forte whipped the faded blue velvet curtains across the studio windows (with his own name appliquéd on to them in a crescent except for the two Ps which had fallen off), the squalor of the surroundings retreated into the dark corners and Rita found herself in a bright, new, perilous world. Mr Forte had escaped after the war in Europe, they said. Escaped what, Rita wondered, looking at his fat, pampered body, his receding hairline, his oily skin. He had an unfortunate squint which made most of the girls in the beginners' class think he was winking at them. They regarded him as faintly ridiculous. His courtly use of language, his thin, reedy voice, his very profession.

'I am a dancing master,' he would declare with untoward pride.

He dressed with meticulous care. A creased white shirt, a dickie bow, a brocade waistcoat. Rita was not used to a man who took such care with his appearance. His unprepossessing looks did not warrant such vain and cautious attention. He would set the stylus down on the gramophone records he used for practice with a plump hand and would move about the dance floor, his arm frozen in mid-air about an imaginary partner. It was not difficult to believe watching him that he was holding a slender beauty with a rose between her teeth.

'Watch my feet,' he would command as if guessing her thoughts, 'and one and two and three and four . . . '

The record crackled at his back. Duly, she watched. She marvelled at how delicate he was on his feet. He turned and wheeled, like a falling feather caressing the air, lost in some distant dream behind his closed eyes. Then the record would end and he would come to in the silence, a plain, fat, balding man called Juicy behind his back because his pupils couldn't master his foreign name.

In her first year, Rita got partnered with Mona Dodd, a tall, graceless woman with buck teeth. There weren't enough men to go around.

'Story of my life,' Mona Dodd muttered as she and Rita laboured across the floor.

Mona played the man but refused to lead.

'No, no, no,' Mr Forte would complain petulantly, breaking them up as if they were boxers locked in hostile embrace. 'Like so . . . ' And he would sweep Rita away, the room a blue haze, his hand lightly settled in the small of her back as he steered her deftly round the room. Up close he smelt of cooking but it was not unpleasant. She loved the sensation of grace and control. And the discipline. She had never worked so hard at anything in her life. It was the closest Rita Spain would ever come to a vocation.

'You're a natural, my dear,' he breathed once in her ear.

She treasured the compliment. Here, at last, was someone who saw *her*, not what had happened to her. He knew nothing of her history – the shotgun wedding, the baby, the kidnapping. He didn't read the newspapers except when they were thrust at him in the barber's shop. The name Spain meant nothing to him, except as a place on the map. Rita felt utterly safe with him. Partly because of his age. He must be forty, she reckoned, his name sounding like a clue. (He was, in fact, thirty-eight.) But also because he was soft and round, his placid brown eyes, the daintiness of his gestures, the sureness of his small feet. And she was consumed with mastering the steps – the wide arc of waltzes, the choppy pertness of the foxtrot, the violent glide of tango.

'You should try the competitions,' he said to her one night as she was gathering up her belongings.

'But Mr Forte, I have no partner . . . '

Mona Dodd had given up after the first term.

'I could be your partner,' he offered.

'Oh no, I wouldn't be good enough . . . '

'On the contrary, carina, it is I who would not be good enough . . . '

Giuseppe Forte had walked into trouble. His two talented feet had danced him into it. He was captivated by a twenty-one-year-old girl, the wife of another man. He knew the dangers and yet he had capitulated. He had not run a dancing academy for ten years without learning where to draw the line. There were women who believed that because he was a foreigner his classes were a front for some furtive kind of lechery. Nothing could be further from the truth. He was a painfully shy man, a man who had never made sense of his adopted country. There had been the problem of language, of course, but he had mastered that. What he had never learned was the easy sociability that was expected of him, the loud heartiness of male company, and the brooding imminence of violence in a divided city. The wet winters depressed him, the rocky isolation of island living. He missed the embrace of a land mass, the comfort of mountains at his back. He had grown up in the town from which Michelangelo had ordered his stone. Carved out of the mountainside, the quarries glistened white in the bleached sunlight, rising like snowcapped peaks above the town square. He remembered fondly the ochre and russet houses, their shutters vainly closed in an attempt to fend off the fine dust that settled everywhere. And the boy that was him sitting on a bag of onions in the Piazza Alberica and hearing through an open window his first two-step on a wind-up gramophone that belonged to the Countess. He never knew why she was called the Countess; the only trace of nobility was her benign madness. A small, bird-like creature, she stood, vacant-eyed and abandoned-looking on her balcony and threw crumbs for the birds and her music flooded out into the chill morning air.

His father had been a stonecarver. Chisel and hammer in hand he carved angels for tombstones and inscribed the names of the faithfully departed in stone. And it was to that trade that Giuseppe was apprenticed and sent abroad to an uncle who had emigrated and had a thriving business in memorials here . . . Giuseppe gazed out at the wet streets, the low grey skies, and longed for a high azure freedom. His feet had saved him. Saved him from a life of chipping away, inch by inch, with blunt, leaden instruments. He despised how primitive it was and how epigrammatic of the human condition, tussling with large lumps of stone and turning them into sightless caryatids or the columns of cathedrals. His uncle died. He sold the business and said goodbye to graveyards. He gazed at his own empire, the garish, ill-lit studio, and did not regret his decision. Only that he had had to travel so far to do it.

He had danced with hundreds of women, a liberty he would never have been afforded otherwise. He had never abused his position of privilege. He couldn't afford to. But he knew that the intricate steps he taught Rita Spain were a form of elaborate courtship like the flourishing of intimate secrets.

If Rita did think of Hazel Mary during this time it was only as a vague premonition, a blur at the periphery of her vision, an angel, liberated and floating high like in the pictures of the Annunciation in the illustrated bible. Tiny, winged cherubs, they gazed down benignly from the corners of the frames, happy and playful. Sometimes they were no more than mop-topped heads with wings attached. She liked to think of Hazel Mary like this without the encumbrance of a scaly, labouring body, all claws and aggravation. An angel baby, a child of flight, gifted in wisdom and foresight. The cream and pink confections Rita wore, the tulle and netting, the satin-covered pumps belonged to this airy world; she thought of these days as golden. Rita Golden's days.

She imagined them aboard the *Queen Bea*, a cruise ship, on course for the New World. Giuseppe and she leading the dancing in the first-class lounge on A deck in the evenings. She heard the applause as the passengers stood back in awe at the glittering arc they made. She swam in the elegant tattoo of their steps, the sooty purr of clarinets, the tinkle of glasses in the balmy nights, the ocean pulling and sucking at the prow . . . that was where the fantasy ended. Rita had developed a fear of water. She would no longer go near the river. On her way home through the dark streets she could hear its hungry lapping at her heels as if it was a creature following her. Its oily depths frightened her; she was afraid of what secrets it might throw up – the body of a baby, for example.

It was the evening that they won the Everglades Pairs Championship. Rita and Giuseppe had gone back to the studios. It was a ritual of theirs to bring their trophies back and put them immediately on display; they could boast a family of them which sat on the mantel in the office at the studios. It was a cluttered room where papers lapped up against the walls or sank faint-hearted on the floor. It always had a distraught air as if it had been recently rifled by a burglar. Giuseppe was moving the cup this way and that anxious to have it plum in the centre. Rita was wearing a turquoise and midnight blue ensemble; Giuseppe had a matching cummerbund. She liked to remember these details and how they seemed to contribute to the overall effect. Ballroom dancing had convinced her how easy it was to convert the world. Her bolero that night, for example, had been made from the lining of a coat that had belonged to Mel's mother. The sea of sequins covered the awkward joins and disguised the fact that part of the fabric had faded. But in the twilight no one saw that; they saw only the quicksilver of movement, a fleeting impression of glitter.

Giuseppe stepped backwards and in the gloom, trod on Rita's foot.

'Oh, my dear,' he said as she stooped and winced. 'I am most terribly sorry.'

He could not bear to see her in pain. He bent down to loosen her shoe – something he had done hundreds of times – but to Rita's dismay, he began to kiss her stockinged foot. A surge of delighted shock went through her. Feeling the touch of a man's lips on those tiny bones of her feet – most used, most neglected – she felt a horrifying wave of desire. She reached down to stop him but found herself instead stroking his hair and finding the pale, bald spot on his crown, soft as a baby's. And she surrendered to his mute and agonised veneration, a man prostrate before her. Afterwards she blushed to think of it, she and Mr Forte grappling together on the floor, the awful foolishness of it. With Mel, she could at least blame her yearning and her own incredulity. No one turns away when a life's dream is offered. But she had never felt more than a vague fondness for Mr Forte – she could not even bring herself now to use his first name. Viewed in the cold light of day, the whole episode seemed outlandish. Why had she done such a thing? She was fascinated and horrified by her own lust. And she was angry with Mr Forte, who had obviously been harbouring these feelings for her for a long time. Each time he had touched her he had been thinking only of this. She thought of him as someone carrying a contagious disease. He had nursed these longings for months. She was angry with herself for not having spotted the signs. She, of all people, should have sensed the wistful power of his pining. His expression of bashful anticipation that greeted her arrival, a sense of grateful surprise that seemed to dog their encounters, the air of tender recrimination that followed any of her unexplained absences. How foolish she had been. And how swift the retribution. This, she realised, was her curse. Her absolute fecundity. Nine months later, Stella Spain was born.

Mel never suspected that Stella was not his. He came home one evening to find Rita waiting up for him. He had got used to finding a darkened house, his father-in-law snoring loudly in the next room and their bedroom abandoned to piles of spangly dresses and pigeon-toed pumps, cards of satin edging, the slender fall of silk. And his wife resolutely asleep. He had grown used to the cold turn of her shoulder. He was a restless sleeper; sometimes he would wake in the night to find he had thrown an arm around her waist or his ankle entwined in hers and he would nuzzle closer to her using sleep as an excuse. But by morning she would have thrown him off and be once more in retreat, her arm clutching the edge of the bed as if she was clinging on for dear life.

'Rita,' he said heartily as he switched the light on in the kitchen; she had been sitting in the dark. He blushed, fearing that somehow she had found out about Greta. 'What are you doing here in the dark?'

'I think it's time, Mel.'

'Time for what?'

'Time to try again.'

She watched him carefully as he took off his jacket and draped it on the back of a chair and remembered how once his presence alone, like this, would have been unthinkable.

Was it the baby that had drained away her once unshakeable belief in him, or would it have happened anyway? She tried to summon up that old feeling, her blind faith, but couldn't.

'You mean . . . ?'

She nodded gravely. For the first time, she felt wiser than Mel, wiser and more treacherous.

Lily Spain, proud grandmother, sat cradling the new baby in her arms, in the kitchen in Mecklenburgh Street. Walter Golden puffed on a celebratory cigar. Mel was boiling water for the feed. Rita surveyed the scene with satisfaction; she had finally managed the impossible − a happy family. Lily stroked the baby's face.

'Funny,' she said, 'but the Spains were never swarthy. I don't know where you got her from, Rita.'

Rita blushed dangerously. Granny Spain was the only blot on her manufactured landscape of happiness.

Giuseppe Forte returned to the country of his birth, to the village in the valley. The ticking summers, the long droughts. He bought a truck and worked for the quarries hauling blocks of stone over the dry roads. His hands grew chapped, his skin weathered. He married a local woman; they had a son who died in infancy. This was what was known about him; the meagre details like an epitaph carved in stone. And when he died in his forty-ninth year − a heart attack in the noonday sun, sitting in the cab of his truck − there was no one in his midst who knew the story of his exile, the northern country, the chill ruins of his foolishness, the impossible love which had afflicted him, the second story of his life.

RITA AND MEL'S final fresh start took them away from Mecklenburgh Street. They were a proper family now, Rita reasoned, and should have a home of their own. She used the growing unrest on the north side of the city to justify the move to her father. There were marches on the streets, not the seasonal waving of flags and banners to commemorate ancient sieges but less ordered parades with placards bearing clenched messages and urgent invocations. It was no longer safe to walk on the north side; proximity to the river automatically meant danger. Trouble, Mel said, was brewing. Rita worried that he had to cross the bridge daily to work, but it was a good job and he had been promoted to deputy manager filling in for Captain Prunty when he was away.

Their flat was small and cramped but because they were so high up – the fourteenth floor – it was full of lofty light. To Rita it was like living in a tree house. She felt unassailable as she stood at the window of the kitchenette and looked down far below at the tiny figures that were people moving about. It was hard-won respectability. She surveyed the domestic flotsam of her life with Mel and Stella, the touching totems of their intimacy, the baby's soft toys, the steaming laundry drying on the backs of chairs in front of the gas fire and she revelled in her sense of relief. The modernity of the place, the shiny false veneer, the wipe-down formica, convinced her that she had made a lucky escape. There were no reminders here of the false start and the lost child. The block was like a vast factory of people where individual lives were reduced to the knocks and scrapes she could hear through the thin walls, the clamouring of the lift, the stony echoes of the communal corridors. Inside it was like a doll's house. She had hung pretty net curtains in the living room. She had cut up one of her old dancing dresses to make cushion covers; they glinted opal and blue. She had made herself over again; the sense of magical conversion made her feel invincible. She did not miss her father's house with its high, dim ceilings strung with cobwebs, the landings perpetually sunk in a watery twilight. It had never been a proper home; it was a shop with a house attached which, like an ugly growth, had distorted all the rooms. Guiltily, she did not miss her father either. They visited him on Sundays but even after a few minutes she could feel the dead calm of his disapproval settling on her which she was glad to shake off. She felt she had made good; he felt she had thrown away her life. Mecklenburgh Street seemed dingy to her now. Derelict in spots, a brown no-man's land. The traders had been moved to another pitch, many of the shops were shut and abandoned. Her father didn't seem to worry about his dwindling custom and the steady decline all around him but Rita was glad to get into the car with Stella on her lap and Mel by her side and drive away from the dark river, and the battered landmarks of her old life. It was not the sick, dizzy kind of happiness she had expected, but it was happiness of a kind and she was glad of it. She only had to compare it to the dazed misery of those intervening years, which seemed as distantly elusive as a bad dream, to be happy. Only the sensations of the nightmare stayed with her. The glare of publicity like the dazzling eye of God watching her, Hazel Mary in the tank, the flames consuming her, and, yes, sometimes Giuseppe Forte. She realised that she had him to thank for all of this but she thought no more fondly of him because of that. She had to reduce him to a ridiculous foreigner with airs and graces who had taken advantage of her. She knew it wasn't true but she realised it was necessary. Any smarting tenderness she might feel, and she did when she remembered him kneeling at her feet, or on the dance floor palming her away then reeling her in, she quickly rebuked knowing how dangerous it could be. If she indulged in such feelings, the next thing she might do would be to blurt it out to Mel and ruin what had been so meticulously constructed. She took it as a sign of getting older that she could handle such subterfuge; it gave her a curious sense of power to have such control over the official version of their lives. She had no troubled history now; she had replaced it with a blameless and invisible present.

Mel Spain was shot at the La Scala during a late-night showing of *The Big Country*. At what point in the plot he was struck down nobody could figure out. It would all have been familiar to him anyway. On a long run he could anticipate the dialogue ahead of time. Rita knew the plots of all the films at the La Scala, not from seeing them, but from hearing Mel recite the lines over breakfast. And then, he would say, rising to enact, John Wayne comes into the bar and boom!

He was shot through the eye; God's peashooting revenge. He was standing in the foyer when the killers struck. There was some disturbance in the cinema, a fistfight between two men. They came to blows because one of them, the taller of the two, kept on shifting in his seat and obscuring the view of the screen for the other man's girlfriend. A patron (Captain Prunty insisted that the customers be referred to as patrons) roamed into the lobby looking for somebody in charge and found Mel slumped on the carpet. His torch was still on, lying limply in his hand, its glare covered by his other hand. A flustered Captain Prunty came on the scene, Mel prone on the ground and a young woman bending over him. His patience was wearing thin. It would not be the first time he had had to reprimand Mel for unbecoming behaviour; he had, once before, come across him and one of the usherettes engaged in a compromising tussle on the back stairs. But this front of house indiscretion was going too far. It was only when he saw the bloodied mess of Mel's right eye as his head lolled back in the woman's arms, his torch falling from his grasp extinguishing its fragile beam that Captain Prunty realised something serious was wrong.

'Holy Jesus,' he breathed and crossed himself hurriedly.

Joey Tate reached for the house lights. A groan went up from the stalls, couples coming to from secret gropings in the dark, the others brutally awoken from the azure spell of a Western sky. A ripple ran through the cinema. The two men who had been raining blows on one another sat down abruptly. There were several minutes of baffled confusion while the film played on looking frenziedly pale in comparison to the real-life drama. Captain Prunty, holding Mel Spain's hand, was embarrassed and exasperated. Embarrassed by the intimacy of the moment, holding Mel's hand futilely – as if that was going to help anything – and exasperated by the din and clamour of the patrons. This sort of thing was bad for business; the kiss of death. He should really clear the place. But they would be looking for their money. He felt it unseemly to leave Mel there, crumpled and . . . dead, for God's sake, in the midst of strangers with a late feature running. And then, luckily, the reel ended and the intermission sign flashed up on the screen. Captain Prunty dropped Mel's hand and bounding down the aisle, leapt on to the stage.

'Ladies and gentlemen, I would kindly ask you to leave your seats. The rest of the show has been cancelled.'

A loud boo came from the front rows.

'There's been a death, here, here in the cinema, one of our staff . . .'

His voice trailed off before he added reluctantly, 'A full refund is available at the box office.'

Mel Spain's last hours were spent in Row K of the La Scala where he had spent most of his life – in the dark.

At first, Rita thought it was a gag. Captain Prunty at the door at two a.m. Mel often talked about the practical jokes they played on the usherettes, locking them into the cinema after closing time, stealing the batteries from their torches. She struggled to get to the door, negotiating her way around the furniture which seemed in the early hours of the morning to jostle in her path, and cursing Mel for having forgotten his key.

'Mrs Spain?' Captain Prunty enquired.

'Yes,' she replied doubtfully.

'Captain Prunty,' he said by way of introduction.

So this was Captain Prunty, Rita thought, putting a face finally to the name. She fully expected that at any moment Mel would materialise from some hiding place beyond her vision.

'Hello,' she said carefully.

'I'm afraid, Mrs Spain, there's been an accident . . . '

He looked shiftily over his shoulder. There were two policemen standing in the shadows but Captain Prunty had insisted that he would break the news.

'May I come in?'

'Of course,' she said and ushered him inside. He closed the door emphatically.

'It's Mel,' he said.

'What about Mel?' She was alarmed now. Was this the stranger at the door she had always feared, the bearer of bad news?

'I'm afraid, Mrs Spain, he's dead.'

This was definitely a joke, Rita decided.

'Dead?' she asked.

'I'm afraid so,' he said shaking his head sorrowfully.

Not gone, not missing, not taken like Hazel Mary had been. Dead. A piercing shriek of laughter came from somewhere in the pit of her stomach. Because . . . because it wasn't a joke. And then she remembered her bargain, the offer she had made to God. Take Mel, she had said, take Mel. And he had. And yet, even while she sat there refusing to believe his death just as in the early years she could not believe his life and hers as one, she knew how fragile their existence together had been and how slender the thread of deceit. And she had always known it would come to this, the distant object of her desire shifting back to its natural position spinning away like a silver token, a coin tossed into the river glinting as it catches the light.

'What happened?' she asked dully.

'There was a shooting,' he said, 'he was in the wrong place at the wrong time. They shot him down like a dog. It was the takings they were after.' He did not add that it had been a matter of mistaken identity. It was Arthur Prunty, police informer, they had meant to kill.

IF RITA SPAIN had seen the two men crossing the play-ground fourteen floors below her on a sunny April day she might have fallen prey to her old sense of superstition. A priest and a detective, unlikely companions unless, as Rita knew, there was bad news to be broken. Canon Power, who had both baptised and married Rita, was a thin whippet of a man with flaky skin and thinning white hair. He picked his way carefully among the knots of children milling on the gravel patch. The first games of the street calender were in progress; skipping, hopscotch, an energetic scuffling that passed itself off as football. He clamped his hand lightly on their heads as he passed, a habit both benedictional and proprietorial. Con Mullarney, bluff and windswept, ambled by his side, glad that for once the news he was bearing would bring no grief. He had seen too often the bloodied ends of things. He thought of the woman they were about to meet, unknowingly working in her kitchen, vacuuming perhaps, or ironing, and felt the precious excitement of these moments, the before moments. As soon as he and Canon Power crossed her threshold, she would be entering the after of her life. It was they who would draw that line; the power of it made him shiver.

Rita had just put Stella in the playpen when the doorbell rang. It was during these mid-morning hours that she missed Mel least. She could pretend as she busied herself around the flat that he was only temporarily absent. Sleeping late in the bedroom, which, with the curtains drawn during the day, always reminded Rita of the artificial darkness of a cinema. She kept them drawn still but she could not recreate the warm, clammy, cave-like air that Mel had given it when he had inhabited it. He had slumbered the hours of a toddler; it had been like looking after a second child. She worried about what he ate; she fretted about his lost sleep.

As she answered the door, she wondered irritably who it could be at this hour. Mrs Loman, next door, for a cup of sugar, or perhaps the plumber to fix the dripping tap in the bathroom. She was no longer in a hurry to open the door to strangers; she knew the perils they could bring. She was not expecting Canon Power. He had called several times after Mel had died and sat in the kitchen wringing his hands and looking at her, doe-eyed, as if his oozing sympathy might cure her. He was here to comfort her, he had said then, but he seemed uneasy with the task and his visits were peppered with aching silences during which she would gaze around the kitchen and consider repainting the cupboards or buying new blinds.

'Canon Power,' she said shortly, hoping not to encourage him. She had a duster in her hand and she effected an air of interrupted work.

'May I come in, my child?'

She nodded glumly.

Another man stepped in behind him. He lifted his soft hat and smiled.

'Detective Mullarney,' he said quietly.

Rita felt a pang. She cast her mind back to old sins. She had been light-fingered as a teenager; she and Imelda had stolen trinkets from a store in town. Earrings on cards, sampler bottles of perfume. She could not take for granted any more the notion that she would not be punished, even for the smallest and most distant of misdemeanours.

155

Reluctantly she showed them into the kitchen where they parked themselves uneasily at the table. She offered tea, but they refused. She stood still, clutching the duster, leaning against the counter.

'Mrs Spain,' the detective started, then shot a helpless glance at Canon Power. Rita wondered vaguely if this had something to do with Mel. Perhaps he wasn't really dead after all, perhaps it had all been a terrible mistake. And for a moment she forgot that he was dead and felt an old stab of irritation; he was never here when he was needed.

'Mrs Spain . . . ' he tried again.

'Rita,' Canon Power said finally. 'We have some news for you.'

Her heart sang with alarm. The last person to use those words had been Captain Prunty. But what more had she to lose, she wondered.

'We are the bearers of good tidings,' Canon Power went on.

Rita eyed him warily.

'We think,' he said drawing in a great breath and then exhaling. 'We think we've found your baby.'

Rita was at a complete loss. What *was* he talking about? Stella was in the playpen in the next room.

'The baby you lost,' Canon Power persisted gently, 'the baby that was taken.' He almost added 'remember?' but checked himself. What mother would need prompting to recall a lost child.

'She has a birthmark, here,' the detective said pointing foolishly to his own chin.

Rita closed her eyes. The room swam in her head. She clutched the smooth rim of the counter.

'Would you like to sit down?' the detective asked, rising and steering her towards his chair. She sank gratefully into it.

'It's a miracle,' Canon Power purred, 'a miracle.'

They had to drag her from the flat, Detective Mullarney literally prising her fingers from each piece of furniture which stood in the pathway to the door.

'My baby's dead,' she kept on saying, appealing to him as he inched her towards the open door. 'My baby's dead, I tell you. She's dead.'

He was shocked by the ferocity of her denials. He had expected unbridled joy; now he felt as if he were apprehending a criminal. She had taken it calmly at first, sitting at the table while he told her about the the childless couple on the other side of the city and their small house on Jericho Street which had harboured its secret for four years. She's quite safe, he kept telling her, quite safe and well. She had nodded dully when he had described the child, her dark hair, the colour of her eyes.

'Hazel,' she had repeated. 'Hazel.'

He had mistaken it for some spark of recognition but he was wrong. She had started sobbing, rocking back and forth. He had reached into his pocket and produced his hip flask. He raised it to her lips but she shook her head and pushed him away. She looked at her hands, splayed uselessly on her lap. Canon Power was hovering at her back, one hand on her shoulder, murmuring 'there, there'. Useless, Mullarney, thought, bloody useless.

'We have to go now, Mrs Spain,' he ventured. He rose and touched her elbow. Canon Power circled around her.

'Yes, of course,' she said dazedly but made no move.

'*We* have to go,' he said more emphatically.

She looked at him blankly. She was no more than a child herself, Mullarney thought.

'Don't you want to see her,' he said taking one of her hands. 'She's waiting for you. Waiting for her mother.'

And that was when the trouble started.

'You're taking me away?' she said. 'I've done nothing, you can't take me away. I've done nothing.'

He caught her more roughly than he had intended. He was afraid he might have bruised her, so brittle did she feel in his grasp. He shook her. 'She needs you, she needs her mother.'

'My baby's dead,' she said. 'She died.'

'No, Mrs Spain, she was given up for dead, but she's very much alive.'

The Cottage Home was a red-bricked building, full of intricate curlicues and a fairytale tower, as if a child had designed it. It stood on a high patch of green near a railway station. Trains rumbled in the embankment below like some vast disturbance of the earth's crust, a groaning prelude to an earthquake. Rita Spain took it as a sign as she stepped out of the car with Detective Mullarney at her side. It was not just her world that had been turned on its head, the very earth was about to succumb to a monstrous upheaval. She was more composed now, he noted with relief. She was carrying her other child, the fair one, clutching her tightly as if she was afraid she might lose her. She had refused to allow Canon Power to carry her so he trailed after them as they stepped into the shiny hallway. A muted clamour greeted them. The cries of children, the clatter of cutlery. It was lunchtime; in the refectory steaming plates of food were being handed down the long tables.

Mother Benildus, a stout woman with a pair of half spectacles perched on the broad bridge of her nose, rolled towards them, beaming.

'Mrs Spain!' she said clutching Rita's free hand and squeezing it. 'You've come for your little one!'

Rita flared angrily. 'There's some mistake, I tell you. This is not my baby.'

'Wait till you see her,' said Mother Benildus linking her as they started to walk down the corridor, 'she's a little poppet.'

Mother Benildus had seen this scene many times before, but in reverse. She had lost count of the number of parents who had accompanied her down this very corridor to

158

leave their children; very few came to claim them back. There were adoptions, of course, but the taint of having been left once seemed to haunt her charges; she watched them leave with a heavy heart. The way they lived here was only a preparation for the big outside world; for the small inside world of families with their coiled-up secrets and hidden disappointments, the Home was useless; it was like trying to land an airliner in a vegetable patch.

'And who's this?' she asked brushing her fingers along Stella's cheek. 'This must be Pearl's little sister!'

Rita stopped abruptly.

'Pearl . . . ?' She turned and looked accusingly at Detective Mullarney. 'See, she's not my little girl. My little girl wasn't called Pearl.'

'It is her given name, it's what she answers to,' Mother Benildus said steering her firmly back on course. 'She will learn another one in time; we all do.'

But for the birthmark, Rita would have chosen the flaxen-haired child with the brown eyes and pigtails because she would have looked well with Stella. She certainly wasn't going to go for the one with bandy legs and a cold sore, she thought vehemently. She watched as they trailed out of the refectory, two by two, the abandoned and the maimed. Ill-assorted clothes peeped out from under their regulation brown smocks. They looked cowed and un-kempt. And she saw the way they looked at her, hungry for recognition. Take me, take me, their eyes seemed to plead. One little boy broke ranks and rushed at her skirts shouting 'Mama, Mama,'. Rita had to look away as Mother Benildus unlocked him from his grasp around her thigh and said. 'No, Robert, not yours.'

In fact, the only way Rita recognised her in the end was that she was the only child not looking for her; she was looking for someone else entirely. She was almost at the end of the line, a sturdy, well-fed child, her nutmeg-coloured hair scraped back into regulation plaits from a pale, serious face, the little mark on her chin. Rita gasped involuntarily. Here was a ghost from her past. But not a ghost. She couldn't relate this live little girl with the stick baby she had brought into the world. She felt the child's size and health as a kind of rebuff, as if she could not have been so if she had stayed with Rita. Slowly she released Stella into Mother Benildus' arms and knelt down in front of the small stranger who stood gazing up at her. Mel's eyes greeted her; she felt a sharp pain and recoiled. She had thought, strangely, that all that would be asked of her was to point the child out, that she could leave then and go home to her simple life of two. But seeing those eyes – like Mel's reproaching her from the grave – she knew there was no going back. She remembered her years of prayerful bargaining for the baby: her trade-off with God. She had wished Mel away, in the same way as she had wished them to be together in the first place, and he had been taken. Now she was coming into her reward. God was honouring the bargain.

But she was being given back a stranger who had been suckled by wolves; who had lived among and been loved by the enemy, those very people who had killed Mel. She came as some gruesome kind of peace offering, a blood sacrifice from the other side, but with *their* blood not hers, running through her veins. A traitor in their midst; a child who lived because Mel was dead. A child who could never be trusted. Rita would never believe that this child and the lost baby were the same. Something had been lost in between. Her own innocence. And in its place a shame, the shame of a mother who, in her heart, had given up on her first-born as dead. How could that baby be anything other than lost, lost permanently? As she stretched out to touch the child's hand, Rita became the mother of three – the lost one, Stella, and now, this one, her third – and contemplated yet another fresh start, her final one. But every fresh start contained a lie, Rita knew, a making over of the truth. To start again, she would have to rip and undo. A stitch of memory here, a seam of longing there, all would have to be remade. For the garment to be passed off as the real thing, the child must never be told that here in the portals of The Cottage Home, her second childhood had begun. How else could Rita make a family of a murdered husband, the child of another man, the ghost of a lost baby and now an orphan of war? She planted her lips on the child's forehead and sealed her new and unknowing future – with a kiss.

PART THREE

I AM REBORN. I have arrived at a bright destination after my long journey. I am swaddled in white sheets, wrapped tightly in them so that when I try to move, I cannot. When I woke I thought one of my arms was manacled but when I looked down it was the grip of my mother's hand on my wrist. I felt bruised and strangely tender, like the survivor of a huge public calamity. Trapped in a dark tunnel, its walls sweating and gelid to my grasp as I clamber towards the light. The hoarse cries of rescuers on the clamorous surface; it is all lights and noise up there. There is a great rumbling, the very earth's crust heaving as if in pain and a boulder eclipses the aperture that I am straining towards. Suddenly there is darkness – and silence. And then from above a tear in the sky and I am delivered from my tiny ante-chamber into a bowl of light.

I tried to raise my head but it was leaden, too heavy for the stalk of my neck. Strands of my hair were plastered to my scalp, the skin of my face smeared and scaly, though my lips were dry and cracked. There was a coppery taste of blood in my mouth. Words crowded on my tongue but only a bubble emerged. It was too early for words, or too late.

'Hush there,' my mother crooned and leaning over me, brushed my forehead with her lips, 'it's all over now.'

Somewhere a baby was crying.

'Where's Jeff?'

My voice, *my* voice! It sounded strange to me, fogged and distant.

A picture of Jeff flashed through my mind, taken on the deck of a ferry. He looks fresh, windblown, healthy, his hand raised in salute. He is on an outward journey somewhere, the perspective is one of departure.

'He's gone,' she said.

I knew then that all was lost.

'Home,' she added.

I thought of our cottage home nestling in an optimistic bend of the road like the curve of a loving question mark. The scene of the crime.

My mother rose and went to the window, standing with her back to me. A bird, full-throated, was singing outside. The branches of a tree scraped against the glass. Not for the first time I thought she was about to reveal something momentous.

'God, but I hate these places,' she sighed. She waved peevishly at the hospital cubicle, the sheeny nylon curtains, the savage insistence of fluorescence.

'Oh, guess what?' she said brightly. 'Good news! Stella is coming home. She booked a flight as soon as she heard . . . '

Stella, Stella! My thick tongue wrestles with her name. Stella, my long lost sister. The baby of the family. I have not seen her for seven years, a fairytale absence. Stella. Reduced to a series of pale blue aerogrammes which sail airily through the letter box and fall with a dying whisper to the floor. The shortage of space means that she writes a sort of telegramese, her life reduced to bare inscriptions. There are oceans and continents between us, half a world. It shows in her tan, the blonde streaks in her hair, in her strange, hybrid accent. I feel pallid and podgy by comparison, and creepily unhealthy as if I had spent my entire life in an institution. I used to envy her looks, the two years between us, her child-star name. Now I envy her flight, her success at getting away. And her new life. A husband and twin daughters – even at a distance, family history makes mocking would-be repetitions. I've never met them but I have the snapshots. The open-air wedding, bougainvillaea and jacaranda clustering in the background, a cloudless blue sky. The timber-frame house with the balcony and a view of the clothes hanger bridge that spans the harbour. The girls with bleached hair in shorts and T-shirts standing under the gum trees. They are so foreign looking, and yet so unmistakeably family. The dark shadows of the leaves dapple their skins; they smile for the future.

It is from this compact world – encapsulated neatly in wafer-thin paper and on shiny celluloid – that Stella has been raised from, her flight this time towards me. Dazed and fragile from her passage across the time zones she moves through the glassy halls of the arrivals terminal. Chauffeurs hold aloft white cards. She will scan them automatically looking for her own name there, or seeking out a familiar face in the crowd. But there will be no one to greet her. I see her driving from the airport through the slush-coloured dawn. The earliness of the hour, the unshaven city streets will add to the penitential air of her journey. She will have to cross the river. Ours is a divided city, a city of tribes, like twins divided at birth. At war, at war with itself. There will be soldiers with blackened faces on the bridge. They will peer in through the car windows, cradling their guns and ask Stella questions; her name, the purpose of her visit. Their questions make me angry. A proprietorial anger for a place I rarely visit unless I have to. A place of debris, stone and rubble, the ruined buildings sagging like flaky confectionery, the ominous, gap-toothed streets.

'They eat their young over there,' my mother used to say.

The river will be in swell as she crosses, green and angry-looking. Sometimes it seems to seethe. Wherever you go, north or south, the river edges in; on their side it leaks into basins, hemmed in by the bleached husks of mills or shipyard docks, peered over by gantries poised like flamingos and the twin gasometers like intricate cathedrals to a sun god. On ours it laps up against the railway embankments and then, dispirited, it peters away, weakly threshing at the weirs downstream. It gives and it takes away. At full tide it trumpets restlessly; in summer when the waters recede, the detritus of the city rears up out of the slime. Battered wheel rims, the mangled frame of a car door, even the red and white cones which mark the boundary on the bridge struggle up from the river-bed in stricken gestures. And the odd bloated body is fished out, of course, the routine casualties of an underground war.

We don't consider it our war; indeed, for us, it is hardly a war at all, more a distant campaign. Mostly, it doesn't intrude. We don't have to suffer the growl of jeeps in the streets or the hectic clatter of helicopters overhead. Shots rarely ring out in the night. We don't hear the ominous screech of brakes as a car bears assassins away. When there are explosions we hear only a menacing rumble. The war for us is a series of small privations, some slight curbs on our freedom (all those questions, for example, which render every activity suspect). There are parts of the north side I have never seen. I know them only from the television bulletins as sites of slaughter, steep streets bearing the names of imperial battlefields and Slavic conquests. It is another world, yet familiar too like the portrait of an ancestor frowning behind glass.

The soldiers will lazily wave Stella on; she is a foreigner, after all, or as good as one. She will drive down the capital's main street, a veritable boulevard, basilica-grey, tinted with thumb-prints of green, the leaves of the sturdy plane trees marching down the central island. The pavements are broad and flagged, a haven for the superstitious. There is a statue of a patriot hero standing with his back to the thoroughfare atop a great, soot-coloured blancmange of stone. At his feet there are angels. Amazons, placid and stony in their regard although one of them, unfortunately, has a bullet hole in her breast, and traitors have been hanged from their giant wings.

Once past the angels, she will be entering familiar territory, the landscape of childhood, our shared history, or rather the history we have in common. One last phantom returning . . .

STELLA IS MORE like a half-sister; the half she left with me is in fragments. The skinny girl with bony knees that is Stella, a limp, blond fringe falling into her eyes, pluckily climbing trees and throwing herself off with a glorious 'whee!', arms aloft as if she might well fly. Teaching her to cycle on the Crescent. It is the only thing I can remember being able to teach her. Holding on to the saddle while she wound herself in under the crossbar – it was a man's bike – and wobbled ahead of me, roaring into the wind 'don't let go!' But I did. Those days in a long-ago June, stretched in the garden sunbathing, lotions applied to a military gleam on her thighs and forearms, a transistor blasting at her ear. Painting her toenails in the bathroom. A paltry store of memories. Less, much less than what I accorded to a sister who never was.

She was the first born, who had come before me and Stella. The Cupid child my mother used to call her. She had brought my parents together; she had made my mother Mrs Mel Spain. My mother told us about the derelict house on Rutland Street where our sister was conceived (since demolished; otherwise we might have made pilgrimages to it), the rotting timbers, the gaping roof, the dying heat of a summer's evening. She confided in us, as girls, as if she were a glamorous, elder sister. She liked us to call her Rita. Her girlishness made me uneasy. I wanted another kind of mother, more serious, less gaily careless, whose life was not such an open book. It was one of my many guilty secrets, wishing for a parent other than my own. But it was more than that. Her delight in her own candour seemed to diminish our sister, as if she were a baby my mother had dreamed up to ensnare the object of her desire, her body obligingly swelling, engorged with lovesickness for a boy she never thought could be hers. A phantom pregnancy.

Stillborn, our sister never even had a name.

My mother called me Moll. A pet name I grew out of, thankfully; now it would make me sound like a revolutionary – or a whore. These days I answer to Mary. Those years as Baby Moll seem lost or like a former life, not attached to this one. As if they died with the name. And there is no documentary evidence. No baby pictures, no handed-down memories of my first tottering steps or the gurgling sounds that would one day become – a word. Sandwiched as I was between losses – my sister's just over, my father's about to happen – such small proud moments seem to have come to grief. If only I could have remembered them myself; there are people who remember being born. Imagine! But not me. It is all a blank.

Our first home, or at least the first one I recall, is a maisonette on the fourteenth floor of the Bridgewater Towers. I remember its shoddy newness and the dusty light at its high windows. Sounds of play drifting up from the playground. From our window, the glint of the river beckoning in the distance, a dagger of silver, a pearl in the gloom of brown spires and green domes. Stella rattling at the bars of the cot. The sounds of my mother working in the kitchen, the hiss of an iron. Whip of cotton, the shy shiver of silk falling from the shoulder of the board, the low crooning of the radio. I imagined her with high, honeyed hair, and a spangly dress with tufts of netting, dancing as the deepening shadows played on the wallpaper in our room. It was green, I remember, with a vertical knotted seam of white running through it, like an agitated river. My mother had hung it herself, inexpertly, so that the joins showed clearly. I picked at them constantly, edging my finger in under the curling edges to see what lay behind. I thought there was another room beyond, the colour of plums, smaller, darker, safer. While we, aloft in our high flat, seemed fragile, like a cradle in the tall branches of a tree, swinging airily in the wind.

The tower blocks loomed around us, frail and bespectacled. Below, far below there was a tarred patch with a listing carousel and a swing frame, its thick chains dangling uselessly. The seats had long since been torn off so we shinnied up the chains instead and hung, grimacing, by our toes from the crossbar overhead. A muted howling came from the underpass. Dogs roamed in packs down there, wild and ownerless, scavenging for food. Near the entrances fluorescent strips bracketed to the ceiling lit the way, but in the depths of the tunnel it was pitch black. I always thought of this spot when the priest intoned the Twenty-third Psalm. *The Lord is my Shepherd, there is nothing I shall want* . . . For me, this was 'death's dark vale'. In the same way as the disused petrol station on the main road was limbo. It was the bleakness and neglect of the place, the weeds sprouting up through the cracks in the forecourt, the forlorn pumps, the derelict pay booth on the concrete island like one last lonely checkpoint between this world and that other one, thronged with the unbaptised, like our lost sister.

As a child I was afflicted by an awful watchfulness. At school, I dreaded the unexpected knock on the door. If an older girl came into Senior Infants I expected to be beckoned forth. A note folded over and handed to the teacher was always a poisoned communication. I would watch as she scanned it, trying desperately to decipher from her features the message it contained. If a stranger walked into the room I believed it was for me he had come. The playground was full of terrors. Leaves would be suddenly swept in a whistling arc across the pitted tar and I would wheel around expecting someone to be there, someone who had caused this flurry. The Angel Gabriel with tidings. There were shadowy places from which an emissary might materialise. The back of the grotto was one such place. It was dark and domed and full of rubbery-leaved shrubs. Here a stranger could stand eclipsed by shadow, reaching out to grab you as you passed. Superstition prevented me from lingering there for long. Instead, I skulked close to the wall near the piled-up crates where our daily ration of milk soured in the sun, or joined frantically in games in the hope that in the confusion somebody else might be taken.

At home people who came to the door unlocked a sensation of recognition as if I had been waiting for them all my life. I remember particularly the man who collected the rent – Mr Hackett. He excited my attention because he came back, time and time again. He was a tall, sallow-skinned man with a moist, almost tearful expression, and bad teeth. He wore a soft felt hat which he carefully took off if he were asked in (he usually was since my mother never had the money ready when he called and would have to hunt down small change in the kitchen). The deliberateness of this ritual seemed to me full of imminence, as if he was about to make some kind of declaration. He would stand patiently in the hallway fingering the rim of his hat with his long, parched fingers. Once when my mother's fevered search was taking longer than usual he produced from his pocket a nougat wrapped in cellophane. I glanced over my shoulder before taking it; we had been warned about strangers offering sweets.

'It will be our secret,' he said putting a finger to his lips.

I popped the sweet quickly into my mouth, balling up the wrapper in my fist to destroy the evidence. I watched him intently as I chewed, certain that now he would reveal some secret to me. He was about to say something else when my mother appeared in the kitchen doorway. I gulped and the sweet went down the wrong way. I could feel it lodging in my throat as I retched to catch my breath. My mother swooped, thumping me on the back and then, suddenly, she swung at me and I was upended. The hall spun around me and I had a bulging-eyed view of Mr Hackett's shoes as she shook me violently. Finally it popped out, a putty-coloured mess on the good carpet. There it sat, like a lie, like my sly, concealed longing for a different kind of love.

She righted me and the hall swung back into place. But the shock of it stayed with me, this violent seizure by my mother's hand, the tipping up of my world as if a storm had overtaken us and all the solid, grounded things had slid away beyond my vision, never to be reclaimed.

Wilful and careless, her retribution seemed to hover insistently. Another memory comes to me. The green-grocer's shop, pungent with bananas. The stout girth of women with straw baskets or string bags queueing patiently while Mrs Pidgeon purred at them from behind the counter. She was a big, blowsy woman, oddly glamorous despite the fact that she hefted crates of fruit around and had dirt under her fingernails from weighing out potatoes. She always wore lipstick and a bright headscarf which swept her hair back from a smooth forehead. I imagined her as some kind of native chieftain, who in her colourful apron and bandanna might well have climbed up trees herself to pick the fruit which appeared in her shop. While we waited, I wandered around the tiered displays touching the dimpled skins of oranges, the caked potatoes still bearing the traces of the earth from which they had so recently been torn, the purple turnips, beaten and battered, the whiskered bunches of scallions with their virgin-looking

bulbs like newly-born infants, raw and screaming. So en-
grossed was I in this strange, uprooted world that when I
looked up, my mother was nowhere to be seen. I lurched
wildly from one set of skirts to another but none bore the
smell of my mother or the slippery static of her frocks. I
blundered on, a heart-stopping panic rising in my throat.
I started to wail. The great bulk of Mrs Pidgeon hoved
into sight.

'There, there,' she said, beaming, as she swept me up in
her fat arms.

'We don't want you, of all people, getting lost, Mary
Spain.'

It sounded strange to me, my own name. It was as if for
a brief moment I had become somebody else there among
the fruit and earth of another place. And then, my mother
rushed in.

'My god,' she cried, 'where did you get to? I looked
around and you were gone.'

But it was *she* who had gone.

Mrs Pidgeon bashfully set me down. My mother wagged
a finger.

'You're *never* to do that to me again, do you hear?
Never!'

I WAS ASHAMED of our loss. That's what it was called. Having no father. It made both Stella and me wary of the species. Other people's fathers were a strange breed, large and threatening. We approached them with caution. There they sat, in sofas, behind newspapers, appearing in doorways they always seemed to fill or on the prowl in other children's houses looking for spectacles, or a freshly ironed shirt. They tinkered with things. They climbed ladders, disappearing into attics so that all we could hear was their heavy footfalls up above, venturing into unknown and dark parts of houses. They lay spreadeagled under cars, only their legs showing, large feet shod in scuffed, lace-up boots splayed outwards. Or they squatted on their hunkers in pairs, their heads twisted sideways, peering under the chassis or into a steaming bonnet.

'It's the exhaust alright, there's a hole here you could put your fist into . . . you're talking shillings here . . . '

I noticed the way fathers talked – the price of things, how they worked, how they fitted together – and how convincingly they traded information. And there were places they went to which seemed to us necessary and mysterious. Pubs, bookie shops, racetracks, where further business was transacted and deals were struck.

Mr Doran, father of Tessie who sat next to me in class, was one I was particularly watchful of. He liked to give us frights, pouncing savagely from behind doors, and he did clowning tricks and funny faces where he pulled back his mouth making his lips thick and slug-like and turning his eyes into smooth Chinese slits. He would lend his body out as a landscape for adventure, cantering about their garden with Tessie on his shoulders, veering wildly over bushes and skirting the rigid arms of trees until they tumbled mightily in mounds of just-cut grass. Tessie would clamber on to his lap, sitting astride his knees as if he were a horse. He would growl and diving at her he would tickle her mercilessly. I would stand back and watch these displays with a fascinated kind of horror. I hated his onslaughts for their suddenness and ferocity, always fearing that one day his attention would turn to me and he would seize me and carry me off, kicking and screaming.

We had Grandfather Golden instead. A stand-in, a sub-stitute. Big, soft-faced and balding, he stood sadly in the centre of his dim, shoe-lined shop on Mecklenburgh Street and served. I remember being brought there to visit, or to be fitted for sandals. The slide and clack of the shoe gauge, the cold dull metal underfoot and Grandfather Golden pressing a thumb on my toecaps and declaring poignantly: 'She should get two summers out of these.' As if he was offering the gift of life.

Watching him kneel before bludgeoned feet, what he seemed to offer was a miraculous cure. He would open the lids of the shoe boxes deferentially and parting the tissue paper, he would inhale briefly the whiffy balm of new leather. He drew each shoe out slowly as if it were a piece of delph. He would hold it delicately between his finger-tips.

'Diana,' he would breathe. He knew shoes by their names. Calypso, Trouper, Pearl.

He stood like a man bereft among his customers' jaded footwear furrowed by grief and lying troubled at their feet, the resilient candour of working men's boots, mud-grimed and thirsting from toil, the stricken elegance of stilettos. In the front hallway there were teetering fortifications of white shoe boxes lining the walls. They were like battlements of babies' coffins. There, I imagined, standing in Grandfather Golden's hall were the caskets of hundreds of unknown babies, their names inscribed on the nether end. I was afraid to be there after dark fearing that the dead children would call out in the night. And one, in particular, the ghost of my sister. I feared that one day I would find *her* name written there.

There were other secrets in Grandfather Golden's house, I was sure of it. Perhaps it was its dimness and the combination of smells, new shoes gone old and Grandfather's own odour, musty and slightly sour. So much of the house was unused; the complete top half was closed off. My mother was oddly insistent that I should recall more of it. It was where we spent the first four years, she would say reproachfully, as if I were betraying her by not remembering. And this, she would say, was your room. I would stand in a cold bedroom with its icy lino and hangers jangling in the wardrobe and peer out at the view. This, I would tell myself, was once the frame of my world. Below the sill, the flat roof of the shop stretched out. On it an upturned bucket, a stick with an oily, black, high-tide mark, a coil of wire. Near the parapet, the leg of a doll. One rotting carpet slipper. A yardbrush, prone. How these things came to be there was a mystery to me. For years, I imagined that someone lived out on the roof, a strange, banished creature who needed exactly this combination of things to live.

When we visited Mecklenburgh Street, Grandfather Golden used to take me to the river. I loved the enclosure of the city, the huddled streets offering, a grimy, decaying embrace, the secretive blind alleys. Oddly, I felt safer there than in our tall tower home where the troubles of the city couldn't touch us. As we walked, Granda would point to the angels in the crumbling architecture, eyeless, yearning creatures reaching out into the air from their columns of stone, perched on pedestals holding lamps aloft, entwined into the arches of the bridge. We would stroll down the quays, hand in hand, or he would lift me up so that I could peer down into the green underworld. I remember still the exhilaration of being so close to the water, usually just a spit on the horizon, and the great sucking sounds it made. As we stood gazing down at the swirling, agitated depths, he would tell me the story of Moses. The child borne by a river. A foundling, abandoned by his mother, left in a basket among the reeds. The story seemed to belong here, to *this* river, to *these* seaweedy banks.

My mother never accompanied us on these trips. Instead she sat in the kitchen behind Granda's shop and sulked. The river itself seemed a source of terror for her, because of its proximity to the other side, I suppose. It was a kind of river blindness. She couldn't get far enough away. Look, she would say disparagingly as we kicked through peelings on the path in the brooding dusk, just look at it, as if Mecklenburgh Street were an errant child dirtied by play. But to me the ramshackle houses, the sad shops, even the litter rustling in the gutters, seemed, as the river did, like the battered but much-loved remains of tales as old as Moses.

Granny Spain also lived on Mecklenburgh Street. In the Mansions – in my father's house there were many mansions, it seemed. The tobacco-coloured flats with balconies at prow and stern, which eclipsed the street's view of the river, were strictly out of bounds on our visits to Grandfather Golden's, a place deemed dangerous, full of rough types, as my mother called them. I remember meeting Granny Spain only once, and that was by chance on the street. It was my First Communion, a brave, bright, blue day of late spring and I am standing in the doorway of Grandfather's shop, shoes curtseying in pigeon-toed tiers to the right and left of me. A street photographer is about to take a snap; he has one of those box cameras held at his chest and he is gazing down as if it were a crystal ball. Granda Golden, my mother and Stella are grouped all around him at the kerb as if it is they who are the subject of a family portrait and I am the observer. It is to be my first ceremonial, part of the official record. A picture for the album. And just as the photographer says 'cheese!' a woman approaches, and then hesitates. A thick-set, silver-haired woman with large, baggy breasts and bruised-looking legs. My mother tried to head her off at the pass.

'Rita, love,' Granny Spain said mournfully.

'Lily,' my mother responded, smiling tightly.

There was some enmity between them which I could never understand. My mother always referred to 'those Spains' as if they had nothing to do with us. I expected somebody fiercer, half-woman, half-wolf, I suppose.

Grannies, like fathers, were a strange species.

'Is this Baby Mary?' she asked as she fingered the stuff of my veil. Her breath smelled of cough drops. 'She's the image of her father, cut out of him.'

'It was me she was cut out of,' my mother said sourly.

'And this must be the little stray,' Granny went on patting Stella's fair head.

'*This* is the baby,' my mother replied. 'Stella.'

'Ah yes, Stella,' Granny Spain said absently, turning her attention again to me.

'Did you know what a precious little girl you are?' she asked. 'We nearly lost you, you know, when you were a baby. You were taken from us . . . '

My mother coughed loudly.

'If only Mel had lived to see this . . . ' Granny Spain's eyes watered. She sank her face into a large handkerchief and snuffled noisily.

'It's not the time to dwell on the past,' Grandfather Golden said pleadingly to her. 'Not today, of all days. A family occasion.'

Granny Spain duly wiped her eyes and ran a creviced hand through the stray strands of her hair. She reached into the pockets of her apron and fished out a florin.

'A handsel for the child,' she said and pressed it into my hand. Silver across the palm. It would bring me good luck, she said.

We left her there, sniffling on the street as my mother bustled us into the house leaving Granda Golden to deal with the photographer. The picture was never taken.

'What did Granny Spain mean when she said I had been taken away?'

'Trust your granny to say the wrong thing,' my mother said.

'But what did she mean?'

'You nearly died, that's all she means.'

It was then she told me the story of my birth. The birthmark on my face, a small rosy blemish which has since faded away, and the cord around my neck. I came into the world almost strangled by my mother's lifeline. A caesarean. I had to be cut out, forcibly removed, a bloodied stump lifted out of her like a part that didn't work, an appendix, a spare rib. And then there was the incubator, a warm, glass tent, the whoosh and gush of its workings like the burble of the womb and me like a tiny, trapped insect inside. A sort of living limbo. For those babies almost lost. A nurse must have taken me there. I see a woman in white rushing through the corridors, hear a beating heart, panic, seizure and flight. A woman, not my mother, on the run, clutching me to her, yet taking me away. To Intensive Care, my first home.

THE LANDMARKS of my childhood are all gone now as if the very city were trying to forget itself. The pot-bellied hospital where I spent my first days, has been demolished. The mysterious streets ironed out into carriageways. Grandfather Golden held out until all of Mecklenburgh Street was levelled around him and the shop stood alone in a field of debris, a picket fence to mark out the boundaries of what was once his enclosed territory, dwarfed by the glinting, wall-eyed gaze of office blocks that had sprung up all around. When his money finally came through we all moved. The house on the Crescent was a big step up for my mother. It was respectability, three bedrooms and a garden. The back parlour was Granda's domain. He sat there, strangely defeated, in his tightly laced shoes gleaming redundantly. He was bad on his pins and seemed to have developed a stoop from his long years of service. He was adrift in our new house, surrounded by the furniture from Mecklenburgh Street which looked old, brown and dissatisfied in our midst. My mother chased him from the fireside with hectoring advice.

'What about a walk, Da?'

And when he obligingly took a shuffle down the crazy-paving path, thwacking at the weeds with his stick, she would frown and mutter to herself: 'Doesn't lift a finger around here and expects to be waited on hand and foot.'

His quietude unnerved her; she took it as reproach. Or she suspected it.

'What have you been telling her?' she would bark at him if she found us together playing draughts, or simply sitting in the parlour steeped in one of his brown silences.

'It's not up to me to tell her anything,' Granda would warn darkly.

'I'll thank you not to tell me how to raise my own children,' she would reply, steering me out of the room. As usual, I would ask Stella, what this was all about. I always felt – and still do – that she was in on things that I had, somehow, missed, as if I were absent for a time, here only in spirit.

'The facts of life,' Stella would say, 'you know, where babies come from.'

I leaf through these memories of childhood as if they do not quite belong to me, or rather as if I do not belong to them. There I am in the midst of family snapshots, smiling bravely for the camera. Seaside pictures, my mother resplendent in a bathing suit that never got wet (she was afraid of the water), an arm apiece around Stella and me, sodden and shivering from spending too long in an icy sea. And Granda, rumpled-looking, a tartan rug around his knees, sitting in a canvas chair set at a dangerous angle in the sand. Whoever took these pictures – some stranger on the beach, I suppose – wielded the camera carelessly so that frequently one of us would be out of frame, reduced to a glimpse of forearm or a disembodied hand. The nuclear family. They remind me now of those Civil Defence booklets dropped through our letter box. Mammy, Daddy and two children, a haunted foursome, eyes popping in the frightful darkness, huddled together beneath an unhinged door laid up against the wall. Our photos seemed to have the same air of rigid startlement. These manuals fascinated me, their lurid graphics of skin burns; the menacing fluff of the mushroom cloud. What to do in the event of fallout. Pile your shelves high with canned goods and hide. Hide out in your own house and wait to be discovered. The threat of The Bomb was much more acute than any of the dangers of the small, real war in our city. When we were children, that hardly impinged. Strange perhaps for orphans of one of its first casualties. My father was murdered at his place of work, a cinema on the north side. We never found out why; mostly there is no why. He was a south sider – these days that's enough. Or it may have been a bungled robbery attempt. Stella was only a few months old. And what age was I, I used to pester my mother, anxious to be part of the drama. You would have been – she would stop, frowning, and do a quick, mental calculation – you would have been, let me see, nearly three. It always bothered me, this hesitation.

I have absolutely no memories of him; it is as if we had never met. And so his death had no import. He belonged to some catalogue of large history like the lost airmen in World War Two or the tomb of the Unknown Soldier. What we knew of him was what my mother told us – his flashy good looks, his swaggering air.

'He was just a boy,' she would murmur, 'just a boy.'

We had a boy father, Stella and I, a boy who would never grow up. It made me feel tender towards him, or what we had of him, his photograph on the mantel, his high bleached forehead, a toothy smile, his gawky haircut.

Our lost sister was more troubling because she was so little documented. My father was dead and so finished with. But there was no gravestone for her so she was consigned to a nether region somewhere. Limbo, Stella used to say authoritatively. But I felt her closer than that. She hovered like a guardian angel on the margins of our lives. I felt her entwined with us like a picture-book goblin melting into the bark of a tree. There, but hidden.

At first, she remained just that, an airy presence, no more than a soft wingbeat of sadness. I sometimes wondered if it were not her I was expecting to materialise when strangers called to the door, or the rustle of trees would become suddenly menacing. But no, I reasoned to myself, she did not wish me any harm. How could she? We had shared the same early home, the cushioned softness of the womb. But where exactly had she gone? It worried me greatly that I did not know. I imagined her an orphan lost in a blizzard, her cries swallowed by the howling of an east wind, trapped in a globe of snow, frozen forever in winter, flurries of flakes falling from its endless heaven. Imprisoned in her lostness. I would wake at night, my own cries mingling with hers, seized by her panic in the throbbing darkness, to find my own world mercifully intact, Stella on the top bunk, the reassuring glow of the street light flooding our room on the Crescent, safe in a world that should have been hers. If she had lived, would I ever have been born? Because I had come straight after her, it seemed sometimes that I was just a substitute, a pale imitation, as if I were the ghost taking her place. Sometimes in the midst of our play, those hours of melancholy make-believe which suddenly seem to run out of steam, the floor strewn with the abandoned corpses of dolls and the faded remnants of my mother's dancing dresses, I would feel a yawning absence of conviction. 'I'm bored,' Stella would say petulantly as if she too knew that I was not quite the real thing. It made me doubt myself. I worried that one night I would wake up and find that our sister had slipped into my place and that Stella, or my mother, would not even notice that I was gone.

And so I invented a life for her, so that she would not want mine, never dreaming that one day I would want hers. I rescued her and I gave her a name. Precious and treasure-like and as far away from my own as I could imagine. Jewel.

JEWEL HAD NOT died: she had been abandoned. For some reason, she would not have been safe with us. Because she wasn't a boy, perhaps. Your father longed for a son, my mother told us mournfully, as if all her misfortunes could have been reversed by a boy-child. I imagined her stealing out at the dead of night and leaving Jewel in a basket hidden in the bulrushes with a note attached. GIVE THIS CHILD A GOOD HOME. There would have been a full moon. The bright tide would have gently borne her away – away to the other side and into the arms of Pharaoh's daughter . . . here is where my story fell down. In my mind the woman who discovered Jewel was not a princess. Even *my* imagination could not stretch to such exotica. No, she was more like Elizabeth, mother of John the Baptist, grown hopeless with the passing years, for whom a child would be a miraculous favour granted by the message of an angel.

I sent Jewel to live in a small, dark house on the other side of the city. She would know the claxen call of factories, the steep terraced streets, chimney stacks spouting steam into a bleached sky. Her world seemed mostly interiors, bound up in sensations of enclosure. Her mother, close by in another room, poised and watchful, who feared for her, who would not let Jewel out of her sight, who would grip her hand to reassure herself that this child was real, who would touch her fingers and the hairs on her head as if she were counting her blessings. I imagined her a sickly child. How else to explain the kind of fearful love she knew? Tubercular, I decided. Weak lungs, a rickety walk listing to one side. Hence her mother's exaggerated care, the enforced warmth, the muffling up against the weather.

Jewel knew the steady thrum of identical days. Her mother rising as dawn breaks, the stoking of the range below, the plish-plash of water in a tin basin as her father shaved. Oh yes, I granted her a father too, with rough, oily hands and a whiff of diesel, a man suffused with a bewildered but grateful reverence for the gift of a late and much-longed-for child. He would come into her room in the mornings to rouse her, carefully putting on her dressing gown and slippers, his breath a warm cloud on the icy air. It was often winter in Jewel's house. His big hands were clumsy with buttons; he often mismatched them. He carried her downstairs, his burly clasp around her waist, her arms tightly clutching his broad expanse of shoulder. Down the bright well of the stairs and along the dim passageway to the kitchen. From her perch on the high chair she would watch as her mother carved a loaf for sandwiches and boiled water for her father's flask, while he spooned out tea from a rusting caddy. I gave Jewel other props that did not belong at home – an oil cloth on the table, a scored and ancient bread board, a chipped enamel teapot. There was a quiet and purposeful air of industry as they worked together; her father's head bowing beneath the palsied sleeves of undershirts hanging over the range, her mother wielding a heavy pan, sizzling angrily, as she bore it to the table. They moved as if in a careful dance for the child on her wooden throne.

My mother always had a crowd in on Saturday nights. There were gaggles of young women on the Crescent, mothers of my schoolfriends. They would go to the pictures and afterwards to the lounge bar in the Plaza or there would be uproarious card parties in the front room to which the husbands of these women would be invited. I recall peering over the banisters listening to their muffled explosions of laughter followed by tense conversations in the hall. There were frequent rows, raised male voices or the impassioned sobbing of women which my mother would airily dismiss in the morning as 'just the drink talking'. The sounds of this unruly adult gaiety would drift up to Stella and me. Stella would often tiptoe down and be allowed to join the party until she fell asleep in a bundle on the sofa. Hours later my mother would carry her back upstairs and carefully tuck her in. I would pretend to be asleep while willing her to pause by my bed and be . . . be what? Be afraid for me like Jewel's mother was for her. To wake me with endearments for fear I might have stopped breathing.

'You're a hardy one,' she used to say, 'you came back from the dead.'

Grandfather Golden kept to his room during my mother's 'evenings'. In his latter years there was a bed set up for him in the back parlour because the stairs were too much for him. He spent his Saturday nights polishing our shoes for Sunday Mass. He would heave out the cardboard chip that held the polish and cloths and would carefully wind open all the tins – black, neutral, ox-blood – releasing their acrid, metallic fumes. He would gouge out a knob of polish and set to with a brush, rubbing at our shoes with vigour, spitting on the insteps to accentuate the shine, then worrying at the leather with a blackened rag. Afterwards he would line them up in pairs on a sheet of newspaper on the kitchen floor ready for us to step into. My mother's were always the last to be filled.

Darkness was Jewel's doorway. At night on the verge of sleep, I would close my eyes and like the step in a dream, the one that finally wakes you up, I had only to take one blind leap to join her . . . a blazing fire. The soft blue-black pile of a hearthrug where Jewel stretched tracing with her finger its curlicued patterns. Against her cheek the rubbed freshness of pyjamas donned after a bath. The house has an evening feel, dusk gathering at the window, lights on but the curtains not yet drawn. The cold chill of the evening invades the house with her father. She makes for the kitchen. There is the scrape of his muddied boots on the red tiles, two stout overalled legs smeared with grease. At eye level the porthole hatch of the range which her father would open from time to time to feed. The sizzling of wet kindling, a burst of flame, the door closes . . .

It was always like that. I was allowed only brief glimpses before I would wake from the dream of her life and find little seams in the air as if the skin of a new world had for a moment been peeled back and then hurriedly sewn up again leaving behind only the transparent incisions.

I would find Grandfather Golden early on Sunday morning blowing on the coals in the kitchen grate while the kettle whistled on the hob, the debris of the night before – the empty glasses, the choked ashtrays – sitting accusingly on the draining board.

'The merry widow's been at it again,' he would say surveying the mess. 'When will that girl ever grow up?'

His exasperation comforted me, somehow. As if he, too, wanted her to be a different kind of mother and was endorsing my wish for it to be so.

GRANDFATHER GOLDEN fell asleep in the August of my tenth year and never woke up. My mother came upon him in his chair in the parlour in the mid-afternoon. She was vacuuming his room, muttering at him, no doubt, under her breath as she worked. My mother approached house-work with a slovenly determination. She pulled the bul-bous machine around behind her (it was called the Baby Daisy, I recall, belonging to a time when household appliances had human names) as if it were a reluctant dog on a lead. Her lack of application was made up for by the amount of noise she generated. She clobbered the legs of furniture with the hose; she stretched it in under things until she hit an obstacle and would then surrender bad-temperedly as if chairs or the sideboard were deliberately thwarting her. She would emerge from these bouts, flushed and dissatisfied, hurriedly dumping the Baby Daisy under the stairs as if she were disposing of a body; there it would lie broken-limbed until she was forced to take it out again. It would have been in just such a mood that she discovered Granda's body, his stillness unremarkable ad-mist the racket she made. She would have shaken him irritably as if he were trying to scare her. Only when she picked up his limp, veined hand and found no pulse there would she have realised. She ran from the house, horrified by the unseemliness of it. Her father, sitting there . . . dead. By the time Stella and I got home from school, the curtains were drawn and a curious hush prevailed which forced us to speak in whispers. My mother sat on the bottom step of the stairs. Even her hair seemed bereaved, falling in wisps around her ravaged face. It was the first time I realised the sheer ugliness of grief. The puffy eyelids, the mottled flush, the messiness of it.

Two men in gaberdine coats came to coffin him. I remember still the ominous thumps that emanated from the parlour as if a tussle were in progress and Granda was putting up resistance. The last we saw of him was his casket like a giant shoe box being manhandled out of the house. I could not quite believe that he was gone. I fully expected that when all the fuss had died down that he would be back again in his spot by the fire. It made me more firm in my conviction that people did just vanish inexplicably, that in a moment's carelessness they could simply be taken away. I was only grateful that once more I had managed to escape seizure.

Our households chimed evenly now, three in Jewel's, three in mine. With Grandfather Golden gone, I felt the tug of her life more keenly as if she were a neglected twin demanding my attention. Desperately she tried to distract me. Like a conjurer she devised daring tricks for me. There were outings, clamorous parades on the streets with the bellicose boom of drums, the screech of penny-whistles, the gilted triumph of banners. They were fearful occasions with their heave and push of bodies but she always had her father's hand to grip and the musty comfort of his Sunday suit. Her mother would wait on the doorstep for their return, worried that Jewel might get lost in the crowd. She was nervous of the throng. She heard menace in the drummed-out messages and imminence in their brassy righteousness.

If I were ill, Jewel produced dangers. I remember coming down with mumps. The crumpled sickbed, my boiling temperature, the lumps in my throat made me prey to a fevered melancholy. Even though I could hear my mother moving about the house I feared that she would forget about me. When she came with hot drinks I didn't want her to leave. I clung on to her hand when she made to rise from the bed not wanting to be alone in a darkened room haunted by Jewel's father who kept vigil, reading from the Bible. Of fallen cities and children rescued from the river. And her stricken mother stood leaning over her; mopping her brow. A recurrence of her old illness. Clogged lungs, a congested chest, a croupy cough.

When I learnt to swim in the public baths Jewel dabbled at the water's edge. She is with her mother. A metallic blue day by the river. She is crouched down feeding bread to the ducks. They are squabbling over the morsels, the gentle ripples they make giving way suddenly to a furious flap of feathers, an aggravated honking. I dogpaddled bravely out of my depth, knowing she was safe.

She is both frightened and delighted by the sudden commotion she has caused, this crazed pecking for crumbs.

'Look, look,' she cries and turning around she loses her balance and slips into the water.

There was a sudden rush of chlorined water in my lungs. I put my legs down and found them wheeling uselessly reaching for the solid ground that was no longer there. I went under; drifted slowly downwards, my hair rising in a plume above like the silvery whiskers of a jellyfish. The water is a murky green. I am with her now on the muddy river-bed. The little bubbles we make rise to the surface, but it is peaceful and silent in our underwater world, joined at last. Jewel and I. And then there is a great thrashing overhead; Jewel's mother is wading in the water gathering up fistfuls of weeds and mud as she claws at the river floor. She scoops Jewel up and carries her away.

Some air, someone hisses, gesturing at the knot of people who have gathered, give her some air. Jewel's mother draws her shoulders up and inhaling gaspfuls into her lungs she presses her mouth to Jewel's. She rubs her chest frenziedly, pummelling her.

'Please God,' she urges, 'please.'

And then suddenly Jewel gurgles and spews up something green and watery. Her mother falls upon her, bending her face close to Jewel's, cradling her sodden head in her arms and whispering into her hair. Her mother has breathed new life into her.

A giant hook saved me, I was hoisted suddenly, gasping and thrashing, to the surface and landed like a fish at the poolside. The lifeguard wagged a finger.

'Stay away from the deep end.'

'This,' said Sister Raphael, 'is one of Mother Nature's wonders. It may not be visible again in our lifetime.'

These words both excited and chilled me, like the notion of infinity. The sky was a pale, frightened blue. It was the sort of day on which the world might end, so still and expectant was it. We carried the bucket out on to the hard tennis court and set it down between the tramlines. We gathered around, an ill-assorted group of twelve-year-olds. The bigger girls, those tall enough to open windows and wipe the topmost part of the blackboard were put standing at the back of the circle. The rest of us, front-row fodder for group photographs, had to squat uncomfortably on the ground. Sister Raphael, a tall, young nun with close-set eyes which made her seem both mean and noble, stood with her hands clasped to her mouth, her fingers forming a steeple of admonishing solemnity.

'The moon will pass between us and the sun . . . '

The bucket shifted suddenly and water slopped around our feet.

'Someone's kicked the bucket, Sister.'

A ripple of mirth ran around the circle; once started it could not be stopped. Hands to mouths, we vainly tried to keep it in, wincing and spluttering into our palms.

'Girls!'

We sobered up.

'The dark body of the moon will be projected on to the sun's bright disc . . . ' She gestured to the clenched ball of light in the sky. 'It will cover it completely, obscuring for *us*, the light of the sun. Only temporary, of course, but for a moment or two, our part of the world will be cast into darkness . . . '

The waters, still agitated, lapped gently in the bucket.

'Hence the word 'eclipse', to obscure, deprive of lustre.'

'What's the bucket for, Sister?'

'Because, my dear, there are some things we cannot bear to see. The fierce light of the sun would blind you if you gazed on it directly, so we look down on its reflection instead.'

We stared into the bucket and waited. The waters darkened . . .

Here is my last memory of Jewel. A hunt for blackberries. The ground underfoot is muddy and wet from a recent shower. Her father towers above her, leaning over her head to pick from branches too high for her to reach. She crouches at his feet shod in wellingtons. She is fascinated by the crenellations of their raised toecaps. Beside her is a bucket housing a rising tide of blue-black mulch. He drops fresh berries into it from his vantage point. She has stopped picking and is instead fingering the pulpy crop, squeezing them between her fingers and smearing the juice around her mouth. There is the soft squelch of approaching footsteps. She looks up. Her mother, headscarved, cries out.

'No, no, don't do that. They'll make you sick. We have to wash them first. Stanley . . . '

The name reverberates. Stanley.

And falls away . . .

Above there was a vast shifting of cloud sulkily reflected in the pail.

'Did you see it, girls? The sun's corona, the bright ring around the edges?' Sister Raphael asked excitedly.

I had missed it; a secret never to be repeated in my lifetime.

THE BLACKBERRY smell of menstrual blood. Jewel tiptoes gently away into the hallucinatory past. By my mid-teens she was no more than a fancy I recalled forgivingly, a cross and garlic for the despair and frights I had ascribed to childhood. At a certain age she just stopped growing, which is perhaps a way of saying that I outgrew her. Once, she had been my equal, but she fell behind along the way, limping in my wake. She reminded me of Kate Burgess, a girl at St Columba's. Retarded, stuck permanently in Senior Infants, she towered above her smocked five-year-old companions. She sat in their midst, wedged uncomfortably into the miniature desks of the nursery or prowled the corridors – classes were not compulsory for her – tall and ungainly, with her pigeon-toed walk, and her glasses askew. She was the school mascot. She led the cheering at our matches; she brought us luck. Katie, our Katie. Everyone called her that as if we all had some claim to her. We indulged her and exploited her in equal portions, passing her forbidden sweets and fizzy drinks – she was inclined to fat – then sending her off on courtly, whimsical errands. Fetch my gym shoes from the cloakroom; tell Clodagh Dunne I'll see her in the bicycle shed. She loved to do messages. It gave her aimless wandering a purpose. She would march forth, frowning with concentration, elbows sticking out and telling anyone she passed the task she'd been assigned. That was her way of remembering. Otherwise, she would end up in the toilets or the assembly

hall like a dazed explorer who has wandered off the map.
Fixtures fascinated her. Taps and stopcocks. Light switches.
Toilet chains. She tested them tirelessly. Cause and effect.
Was she aware of the passing years, I wondered, the growing disparity between her size and our progress? In my final
year Kate Burgess was four inches taller than me but still
turned rope on the playground. She is probably still
there, for all I know. A woman-child playing in the sand-
box.

I remember the idleness of adolescence as if I was recuper-
ating from a debilitating illness – called childhood, perhaps. A succession of monastic-like interiors. A round of
cell, refectory and cloister. It was as if the world had been
roofed over and outside, for all its airiness had been reduced to an arcature of sky and a bare quadrangle of green
glimpsed briefly through a colonnade. I felt muffled up, a
patient with a cold, troubled by sluggish limbs, watery
eyes, a bulbous nose. Examining my face in the mirror I
found it strangely blurred, the features stranded in growing fields of flesh. Puppy fat, they called it. I seemed a
stranger to myself as if in the clutches of a volatile other,
who was irritable, easily riled, hard to please, who sat with
arms folded and demanded entertainment. It was she who
paced restlessly in my room, going to the window, picking
up a book, throwing it aside, flinging herself on to the
bed, moved by an imperative which vanished as soon
as she acted upon it, while I was happy to spend hours
in absent rumination, a kind of mental sleepwalking,
until I would be called forth and made to account for
myself.

I wake from this torpor in my final year at school and find
it is the world that has been transformed, not me. Stella is
already a young woman, round of breast, her long mane of

hair tossed wilfully over one shoulder, looking preposter-
ously overweaned in a school uniform. She bursts forth,
fully grown, a neat aggregate of my parents – my mother's
fair, pretty looks, my father's rakish height. Where has she
been all these years? A sleeping beauty suddenly roused.
But, of course, it is I who have been absent. I had been
plodding on with my books presuming that she was following on behind me. But the very things I loved about
school stifled her. The regimen of bells, the dress code, the
order of it, these appealed to me. I liked the feeling that
there was somebody reliable in charge. It was the one place
I had no doubts about; I certainly belonged there. I am
nostalgic now even for its battered geography – the loose
parquet flooring, the scarred desks. Long corridors, wood
to waist height on the walls, high sash windows. Below,
the asphalt courts glinting as if they were paved with silver,
rain drumming on the roof of the bicycle shed. The smell
of saturated gabardine drying in the cloakrooms. From the
classrooms the low rumble of irregular verbs. Funny how
my memories of it are as the interloper, the girl put out on
the corridor as punishment, although that is not how it
was. It was not that I was a remarkable scholar, but I kept
my head down – a practice of old – and it was mistaken for
application. More often it was daydreaming and an earnest
wish not to become the centre of attention. While all
around me girls saluted the air with their hands hissing
'Sister, Sister', I slunk low in my chair and prayed not to
be noticed. I wanted only to be invisible, to be passed
over, left alone to blend in with the crowd. I had a horror
of being singled out. There were times when I would
catch a teacher looking at me appraisingly with something approaching grudging regard, as if a vague sense of
distant celebrity hung about me. They looked at Ita
Manners in much the same way. Ita Manners had been to
Lourdes and left her crutch at the grotto, though she
still wore calipers and walked with a limp. I put it down to
my widowed mother, the pitying allure of orphanhood. I

suspected they got the whiff of the workhouse. I seemed to get extravagant – and unasked for – praise for being mediocre. For even making an effort. Less seemed to be always expected.

'See!' Thirty-five resentful faces would turn on me.

'*Someone* did her homework despite the power cut.'

My orderly copybooks, my neat handwriting, these were hoisted up and passed around like pieces of incriminating evidence.

'There's one composition I'd like to read aloud . . .'

These were words I grew to dread. No wonder Stella tired of it.

'Oh,' she would mimic, 'you must be Mary Spain's sister!'

Stella left school at sixteen. If Grandfather Golden had been alive, he would have protested but it was my mother's rule that went now. She worked in a succession of jobs. A dry cleaner's, a bookie's shop, an undertaker's. It didn't seem to matter. What did matter was there were boys. Disembodied voices at the end of the phone who would materialise at the door bearing only their first names. Paul, Frankie, Raymond. I see them now as a composite, curly-haired, beefy, with a certain shy kind of swagger. There they stand, hands lazily fisted in their pockets, narrow-eyed and sullenly defiant, cigarettes dangling from their lips. I looked at them and saw my father. This was the kind of boy he must have been. My mother took much pleasure in their ardour; it was as if she were being courted herself. And they, in turn, *loved* her. They lapped up her coy gaiety as she hailed them from the kitchen – come in, come in. If only all mothers were like this, I could almost hear them think, as they brushed past me in the hall and straight into my mother's showgirl embrace. They shared their cigarettes with her, lighting hers with those snappy gold lighters that were the fashion then. Meanwhile, upstairs, Stella would be coolly dressing. I remember her wardrobe from that time. Peach-coloured dresses to the knee, granny-print skirts to the ankle. Scoop-necked tops, faded flares. Small bead handbags, sling-back shoes. And lots of careful make-up. Eyeliner that didn't show; lipstick with a faint pearly gloss. I see her casually clipping on earrings as she backed out of her room where clothes dripped from doors, mirrors, picture frames, and spraying perfume between her breasts as she hurried downstairs. Where had she learned such tricks, I wondered. She had passed me out when I wasn't looking. She was the elder sister now.

My mother would sit up into the small hours waiting for Stella to come home from parties or dances, not to berate, but to share in the whispered confidences of the night. I would hear them in the kitchen, laughing delightedly together, then hushing one another extravagantly like . . . like sisters, while I lay wakeful. They turned me into an irritated mother, sick with fear at the hours they kept and disapproving of their flightiness. Sometimes I would bang on the floor to quieten them (this behaviour was more the territory of tyrannical grannies) or I would stumble downstairs, gummy and cross with sleep. Their animated chatter would halt immediately as if they were discussing adult secrets I was too young to understand. As I clattered sulkily around the kitchen, my mother in dressing gown and hairnet would slink disconsolately to bed; Stella would sweep up her earrings and her discarded shoes and I would be left alone with the lipstick-smudged cigarette ends wilfully bent and stubbed out, the curdling coffee dregs, the whispers of sex. I felt both excluded and abandoned. The truth was I was terrified. This version of the world which my mother and Stella offered was too calculatingly female. I feared I would never manage out there. The lopsidedness of our household constantly reiterated itself. I longed for the saving grace of Grandfather Golden or my long-dead father, some male ballast, some man, any man who would show me that this was not the only way.

I SWAPPED ONE institution for another. From school to hospital in one swift move. My mother was perplexed at my choice.

'A nurse, for god's sake,' she said, 'all those sick people! And you were never a good patient.'

She is terrified of hospitals; she sees them as factories of disease as if the very buildings devour people. I like their scale, their vastness, the urgent sense of vital business going on. Life and death at the same time. And the work itself which demands such careful vigilance. Night duty when the busy clamour of the day has died away and every sound is magnified. When the thrum of plumbing, the creak of a door, the ticking of a floorboard becomes significant, slyly asserting itself in the huge silence. When the human voice becomes a sacrilegious boom. And it feels like we are aboard a doomed liner, going down. I listen then intently for my patients' breathing, those shifts and whispers smuggled into the night. I go up close to them. I am tempted to touch them (I touch them all the time, of course, I take their temperatures, I give them bed baths) to push back their hair from their foreheads and croon to them. I curb the temptation; it is not seemly. I distrust myself. Who would want to wake up to a veritable stranger hushing them, trying to inch some feeling from them while they sleep? Not me.

Jeff was brought in with gunshot wounds. Trouble, when it comes, comes in waves; there are weeks of sporadic shootings and revenge killings and then like a fever, it dies away. The calm is often more eerie than the storm. We listen more closely to the news bulletins then; it is during just such a calm that the whole thing could explode and engulf all of us, both north and south of the river. Through the war we have acquired new specialities – shrapnel injuries, false limbs. The wounded are often taken to South Side General. I was on duty in Casualty when Jeff arrived. A random victim. In the wrong place at the wrong time. His belly gaped; a towel had been stuffed into the wound to staunch the flow. This was our bloody beginning; not unlike the end.

He was taken to theatre for emergency surgery. I remember the journey through the dull, glazed corridors, the blurred white squares of light overhead which he kept on counting to keep himself awake, while I held the IV pouch overhead. He panicked when they came to put him out. It is like a rehearsal for death, volunteering to go into the darkness alone. I held his hand, simply that. A hand that anchored him, secured a place for him in this world, I suppose. And I was there when he woke, bleary-eyed from his long journey. He smiled sheepishly.

'Maybe,' he said, 'when all this is over . . . ?'

I watched him avidly during his convalescence, indulging in a kind of lovelorn surveillance with a mixture of appalled gratitude and empirical curiosity. So this is what people felt when they talked about infatuation. At that stage I didn't dare use a word as presumptious as love. The fact that he was in danger gave my feelings a suitable urgency, though it seems absurd now to think of him as doomed. The first time we made love was in a broom cupboard on Ward D; it smelt of starch and gumption. We grappled with one another like terminal patients with

203

nothing to lose, tenderly consumed by a startled kind of innocence. It was hot and urgent, yet even so I could not surrender to it completely. The memory of a child conceived in a rotting house on a summer's evening invaded. I felt the pebbles that must have left their dimpled imprint on my mother's thighs. A grating soreness between her legs; astride her, my father would not have waited. A bruise on some soft fleshy part (I cannot imagine him being gentle; I cannot imagine him at all). And afterwards her swollen mouth and smarting cheeks as she gathers up her scattered clothes – how is it that after sex, it is the blameless underwear that seems soiled? It was only when Jeff pressed his lips between my legs, labouring like a suckling child, his tongue divining a cleft until it struck a spring and a joy seeped out, a joy so bleak it was akin to desolation, that I was released into his world, a battleship-grey dawn, the whine of sirens, the spat of gunfire, the crash of soldiers' boots, the splintering of wood.

He was from the other side of the city. Perhaps it was that fact alone which made our association in those early days into something illicit and dangerous. That and my circumstances. I was in the nurses' home at the time. The corridors were patrolled by nuns checking to see if the toilet seats were up, or so the joke went. There was a lot of smuggling going on in the form of live cargo – men disguised as brothers or cousins – and Keystone Kop scenes on the fire escapes as, half-dressed, they made their getaway at odd hours of the morning. I remember the dishevelment of my small room after a weekend spent in bed together. Tea trays on the floor, the Sunday papers dismembered between the sheets, the jet-lagged sense of time. Going to sleep when dawn was invading the room and waking to the muteness of the Sabbath, rain dreeping from the sills.

I would rise early on those mornings I was on duty and, emerging in an ironed uniform and starched cap out of the cramped cave we had crawled into, I would set out across the forecourt to the hospital smug in the secret knowledge that I had left a man behind, and that he would still be there by the time I got back, having barely stirred in the crumb-ridden bed. These routine habits, the animal comforts of intimacy were new to me then. Now they seem distant and outlandish, like the rituals of an abandoned religion.

Unlike Stella, I didn't bring him home for inspection. It pleased me to think that my mother knew nothing about him; it pleased me even more to think that she didn't know that he existed. He was just one more secret I was keeping from her. She would not have approved. I was consorting with the enemy; the very people who had killed my father. We should cut them off and set them adrift, she would say, as if we were not adrift already.

So tell me, I can hear Stella say, what was he like? I hid him from her too. I liked his hands, sturdy and graceful, and his russet colouring like a fallen apple. His endearing freckles, a perfect set of teeth. When he smiled it was like watching the sun come up in his face. How hard it is to sum up the beloved. It is as if we get so close we cannot see. Like viewing a cathedral, it is a simple cornice we remember, the blue of a mosaic, the mother-of-pearl inlay. That is how I will remember him. Tantalising fragments of a lost dream.

Stella stole away into the night, or that's how it seemed. She stealthily gathered her papers together, visa and passport, and booked her passage. I arrived home to the Crescent one evening to find the house in disarray and my mother in tears.

'She's going,' she said, 'she's going away. Another one of my babies . . . lost.'

I was shocked. Stella had been keeping things from me.

'Talk to her,' my mother pleaded with me. 'She'll listen to you.'

But why should she? I was no better than a stranger, someone who had been billeted with her. She had escaped from me a long time ago.

'Don't you start,' Stella said eyeing me menancingly. A suitcase gaped on the floor. Dresses wept from the bed. 'I've had enough hysterics for one day.'

'But why?'

'Just listen,' she said. My mother wept noisily in the next room. 'She wants to live my life for me.'

'No,' I protested.

It had never struck me that Stella might have ambitions for anything other than the round of young men, and the gleeful confederacy with my mother. She plucked up a pale green sweater and held it up against her.

'What do you think? Too heavy for where I'm going.' She tossed it aside.

'No,' she amended, 'she wants to *have* my life.'

'What do you mean? I don't understand.'

'Surprise, surprise! Where have you been all these years, Moll?'

I was startled for a moment. By the baby name, firstly. An appropriation of some knowledge of me she had once owned. And then by the accusation. The accusation of absence.

'She had her turn and she made a mess of it. Now she wants my turn.'

'But I thought . . . '

'What did you think? That I enjoyed watching her act like a teenager, competing with me all the time?'

'Well, no . . . ' I started.

'You opted out so she pinned all her hopes on me. She wants to be Rita Golden again as if none of this, you, me or even that fucking baby that forced her to get married, had ever happened.'

Her ruthlessness amazed me.

'I think she made it up, you know?'

'Made what up?'

Stella's capacity for absolutes had always alarmed me. Her easy delivery of neat resolutions. Things I had been mulling over for years, *she* seemed to have solved.

'That baby,' she said, sneering. 'The Cupid baby.'

'No!'

This was private territory she had no right to invade.

'All in her head, I reckon. Pure fantasy.'

I tried to play for time.

'Would you not wait a bit? Let her get used to the idea.'

I knew I was pleading, not for my mother's sake, but for my own. I was afraid of being left alone with her. And I suspected my mother's panic was not just about Stella's departure, but the fact that she would be left alone with me.

'What's the point? She won't like my going no matter how long I wait. No point in prolonging the agony. Anyway, there's nothing for me here. Look at the place.'

She gestured to the window. A light summer drizzle was falling on the Crescent. The apron patch gardens were lush green and glistening. Beyond, out of sight, the distant city, the pearly glint of river and the racket of gunfire. It was a volatile time, marches on the streets, angry mobs besieging public buildings and setting them alight.

'But this is all so sudden . . .'

'Sudden to you, maybe,' she replied tartly.

She heaved the suitcase on to the bed.

'Do you know what she asked me when I said I was going?' She laughed wryly. 'You're not pregnant, are you?'

My mother and I saw her off. The mail boat at dusk, the twin piers hugging the harbour. The lighthouse at the edge

of land blowing tantalising kisses of light. And Stella leaning over the rail and waving vigorously as if to dispel the
ghostly defeat of other losses.

'So long!' she hollered above the din of farewell and the
clank of iron chafing against the quayside. Her hair
whipped about her in the wind. 'Wish me luck!'

JEFF AND I were married on a winter's morning. Grey clouds brooding with snow hugged the steeple as we stood shivering in the churchyard. His mother and father crossed the river for the ceremony. Both his parents were living – I attributed this to some great carefulness of Jeff's affection; we, on the other hand, consigned our loved ones to early graves or great distances. I thought at the time that they were adopting me and the church ceremony with its elaborate rituals of handing over and surrender seemed to endorse this. Now, of course, looking back on it, I see that it was I who adopted them. His mother was a thin, stately woman. I imagined her as the loyal wife of a disgraced monarch who had abdicated for love, though the image did not hold looking at Jeff's father, rumpled and gamy, a man who seemed destined to be errant even when he didn't have a drink in his hand or an arm around some woman's waist. I remember meeting them for the first time. They lived in a small, terraced house on the north side, in the shadow of the shipyard, on a street that rose grimly, steep and inevitable. The worthy poor, Jeff said as we drove through a tangle of red-brick lanes, strung across with washing lines. Women gathered at the street corners, children skipped on the flagstones, men stood in their shirt sleeves in doorways pulling on cigarettes. Banter flew across the narrow streets, bunting flapped from the eaves. A dizzying sense of familiarity assailed me as Jeff pointed out the rusting gasometers, the poised cranes. But then I had been looking at them all my life from a distance. To drive through these sodden streets, punctuated by derelict patches and the gable ends of burnt-out terraces, was like being in the territory of dreams, a private landscape suddenly populated. The street names leapt out at me – Babylon, Macedonia, Jericho – like a ruined and cryptic version of home.

I kept on expecting to meet somebody I knew.

The Speights welcomed me with open arms. Mamie, serving tea in the dim back scullery, appropriated me as if she had known me all her life.

'Spain,' she said musingly when we first met. 'A real southern name, that. Rings a bell, somehow.'

'That usher who was killed at the La Scala, oh, must be twenty odd years ago, he was a Spain, wasn't he?' Jeff's father said.

'My father.'

For a moment, he was there. Young Mel Spain, in uniform and cap, a ghostly witness summoned and giving us his blessing.

'I have no memory for these things,' Mamie confided.

I was like the daughter she never had, she said.

'We longed for a wee girl, but it wasn't to be . . . I had several misses, after J.F.'

She used his initials; it was a family joke. He had been christened John Francis, because of a mix-up at the church. Two babies, one of them a girl, arrived where only one was expected and the priest had mistakenly baptised him as Frances. His father decided to keep the unwanted second name. It stuck, like the ghost of his sister who had never come.

'You never forget them, you know, the lost ones,' Mamie said. She observed a moment's silence.

For the first time in years I thought of Jewel, dark companion of my childhood, because, I suppose, I had finally ended up in her territory. It was to these streets, to just such a house, I had banished her. As I looked around its cramped rooms and Mamie's scallop-edged net curtains, the carefully crocheted antimacassars, the good china brought out in my honour, I felt the sharp shock of recognition as if I had been here before.

Jeff's father bent to the stove and opened its creaking door.

'Fire's nearly gone out.'

He tramped heavily to the back door and stepped out into the dank yard. The shipyard hooter sounded three times calling the men to work. He heaved in a bucket of fuel.

'Glad that's not for me,' he said as he piled the turf into the glowing porthole of the stove. Jeff's father had been a shipbuilder. In the good old days, he would say, when there was plenty of work.

'The *Queen Bea* was built here, did you know that? A beauty, she was, a proper cruise liner . . .'

'Which went down with all aboard, if you remember,' Jeff said.

'Don't get him started,' Mamie interjected. 'Do you know all I remember of those years? Loads of grimy laundry and the stink of grease. Good old days, my eye.'

Jeff laughed fondly. And I joined in, glad to be inheriting their nursed grievances and small rivalries because for once they did not implicate me. For the first time in my life, I felt entirely blameless.

Scenes from a cottage home. I am standing at the kitchen window watching Jeff bowing to a spade, wet earth on his boots, his sweater the colour of rotting leaves. It is autumn, a day drenched with recent rain. He is building up a pile of sodden twigs and branches. It is slimy underfoot where apples have fallen and decayed, and I am wondering if the bonfire will ever catch. It may smoulder and smoke a little, trying hard to be a flame, but it will never blaze.

This lack of belief seemed to dog me; I could not trust to happiness, it seemed constantly endangered. I thought death might take him away from me. I feared the knock on the door, men in uniform doing their official duty bringing news of a calamity. A car accident, the sudden swoop of illness, another shooting. His work took him to the north side often; he was a police photographer. He took pictures of the dead, the victims of snipers and bomb-makers. A steady clientele, he used to joke. I could only imagine what horrors he saw. From the television I knew about random death on the street, a corpse in its own blood, discreetly shrouded by a sheet or someone else's coat. But Jeff drew back the shroud and looked at it straight on. There would be bloodstains sometimes on his clothes, the blood of strangers. He crossed the river bearing with him the spoor of other people's bone and gristle, and worse, the ghastly images of the dead. I feared for him; it was a version of closeness, I suppose, this sense of fear for the other. But it felt more like a haunting, a rehearsal for the dreaded loss.

I see us together, Jeff and I, busily carving out domestication, the rooms smelling of drying paint, the gnawing sound of wood being sawed in two. We put up a ceiling in the kitchen. Tongued and grooved. Tongue-in-cheek, I used to call it, in error. I remember handing the planks to Jeff as he stood, arch-backed on a trestle, hammer in hand, as if all our efforts in retrospect were just mere contortions. Each lath had a lip which fitted into its neighbour's cleft to form a sky of pine overhead. But there were flawed ones in the batch that wouldn't lock together. We dumped them in the coal shed, blackened and abandoned.

There were days of sunshine like tender gifts offered up merely to please us, bright openings of the sky full of benediction as if we were being indulgently forgiven. And there was the comfort of skin on skin, the quiet miracle of coupling and its sated aftermath as if we alone had discovered some fevered secret, that two can become one, I suppose. Or that two can never be one. And then, briefly, there were three.

The baby was a mistake. Neither wanted or unwanted. Not planned, in other words. I couldn't believe it. Somehow, I had always thought it would be difficult for me. I thought of myself as one of those women who would have to labour for a child, engaging in a long process of trial and error. We could always adopt, I thought, an orphan from the north side, perhaps. I liked the idea of providing a safe home for a sad child. I relied on the notion that some physical obstruction would be found, some part of me that wouldn't work, a flaw in the reproductive organs. For years, I thought of myself as barren. So when a baby edged its way into our lives it was like an unsought-for miracle. And I kept it a secret.

I don't even know when it was conceived. Was it that crisp, clear night, a single star in view, a shivering of trees at the window, or that Sunday morning, still indolent with sleep, the sheets in a tormented tangle beneath us when Jeff, moaning softly as he came, called me his precious, his jewel?

She rose from the ashes of the north city, and travelling by night, she crossed the bridge and became a living, breathing child, clamouring for my attention. I caught fleeting glimpses of her in the street. A dark child grasping at the air for a mother's hand. I saw her on buses and trains, a small face framed in the window, waving absently at the world. She appeared in the aisles of supermarkets, perched regally on a trolley, although when I hurried to catch up with her I would find that it was not her at all. Worst of all, her cries would wake me in the night. I would sit bolt upright in bed and hear her sobbing; she had woken from a nightmare and wanted to be comforted, to be reassured the bad dream would not come back. I could picture her, a small girl in pyjamas, in a dormitory somewhere, an institution of some kind, coming to in the darkness, howling. It was a high-ceilinged room, with varnished rafters, and light coming in from the long uncurtained windows. The white bedsteads all around her gleamed dully in the night. Hurried footsteps approached. I expected a mother, but it was instead the heavy tread of a large nun in slippers, beads clacking . . . Only then I realised that Jewel had no mother. It was not she who had been lost, it was her mother. And she was calling out for me, not from the dim recess of the womb or the dreamy distant city I had housed her in, but here in this world, in *my* world.

I tried to explain it away. The hormonal tricks of early pregnancy. The nameless fears of one who is carrying something so small and fragile it seems impossible that it will survive in a world full of perils. I was granting my baby personhood before its time, giving it gender and a fully-formed body and a host of already garnered memories in which I had no part. Perhaps all expectant mothers did this, I thought, to render the growing foetus real, to rescue it from being just an imminent notion. A kind of superstition that if the baby is fully imagined, it can make its way down the birth canal, struggling to grasp the life already dreamed up for it. But the trouble was that I knew I was not creating dreams for this secret baby within, I was being revisited by the dream of a child I had created so long ago that I was amazed she still remembered me. I had left her behind, a little girl, *my* little girl, and now she was claiming me back. There she stood in a line of smocked orphans on parade waiting for the glassy door at the end of a long, polished corridor to open and a young woman to arrive who would single her out from the ranks of the disowned. And that young woman was me.

HOW CAN I explain this madness? She was real, she was there, I swear it. She had been there all along, fostered out to parents of my choosing, living a life not her own and waiting for this moment to be restored to me. The baby within was but a pulse beating, a mollusc of flesh, lightly embedded on the ocean floor amidst cities of pebbles driven by the swell and tangles of swollen-podded sea-weed, ochre and brown. But Jewel, Jewel was fully formed, a child who was part of me, whom I had nurtured and loved and thought I had lost. How could I have abandoned her? She lived and breathed, she stalked my dreams, she begged for my attention. I could not turn my back on her. She was my firstborn, my only child. No other baby could be allowed to take her place.

Jeff is the stranger who arrives in the middle of the night-mare, the man in the white coat, all reasonableness and calm, who steps across the bloody threshold and tries to restore order. There is the conjugal bed, steeped in blood, the sheets tormented as if the witnesses to violent love, a woman clawed by the pangs of birth, screaming. His first instinct is that she has been attacked, that someone has literally tried to slaughter her in her bed. He searches the rooms for evidence of an intruder, a forced lock, rifled drawers, a weapon that could have inflicted such wounds. And finds it in the knitting needle beside the bed. He tries to stem the flow of blood but cannot staunch it. He talks to her through her delirium which has transformed her silence into a kind of exultance of pain. She rides on waves of it, like someone possessed, exhilarated by the sting of seaspray and the thunderous roar of the sea.

'What have you done?' he shouts at her.

At this stage it is merely a question. Only after the ambulance arrives does he ask again, sorrowfully, the blue light flashing across his face, the scream of a siren drowning out her answer.

'What have you done?'

'You should have told us,' my mother says rubbing my hand regretfully. She has never given me such attention. 'About the baby, I mean.'

'It was a secret.'

'Poor Jeff, even he had no idea.'

My secret, it seems, is safe. His parting gift. He must have told her no more than that this was just another lost baby.

'There'll be others, you'll see. After all, I had you and Stella after my first one.'

But she is wrong. There will be no others as compensatory gifts.

I am a *tabula rasa*, born again, with my history excised, cut out of me. Vacant and bleakly empty, only now am I ready to begin my life. There can be no future with Jeff. I am unfit to be with him, unfit to be with anybody. Cursed, as I am, by a savage reversal of the natural instinct. I have killed his child by my own hand. I struck out and tore away the very stuff of dreams, the cringing flesh and blood, the throbbing pulse. And all for a phantom, a wilful sprite, a demon, perhaps. I will return to our cottage home. Alone. A criminal. Will it be haunted too? That bed, those sheets? Will I wake in the night and hear the cries of the creature I expelled there in a mess of a blood and sweat? When I open the wardrobe will it be filled with ghosts or just slack-limbed clothes? Will the drawers house murder weapons, or mere household implements, useful items for opening tins or uncorking bottles? Will there be a secret existence hidden there, lurking in the corners of the rooms or hovering airily with promises? Or will there just be the hard, bright, concrete things of the world saying, now, live with us? This life, a life reduced to one.

Jewel? She is gone. I try to summon her up, the little girl in the orphanage waiting in line but I cannot. The corridor is empty. The glassy door is shut. Dust motes swirl in the weak light and there are echoes of children at play outside. But Jewel is not among them. I have been left in peace, liberated from the shackles of a child that never was. A dream child.

I was wrong about her. Blindly mistaken. Those ghostly memories I ascribed to her, they're mine. They were always mine. Memories not of this life, but of a life before. Before birth. Not the scaly, red, wet burbling of the womb. No, before that even. The Garden of Eden. And my first parents. Adam and Eve. Already under threat of expulsion but hanging on to the dream of happiness. Eve, knowing she has stolen her joy, savours it precisely because she knows it will all come to ruin. My first mother, consumed by an illicit love. And Adam, ignorantly happy in the hours before banishment. *My* banishment. I wonder if my Eden still exists? Or has it turned to wilderness without me? You see, I have resorted to biblical metaphor. But it is all I know. And so much more exotic than the literal truth. A mother exasperated by my difference, a father who exited too early, a sister who keeps her distance. I almost drowned. Drowned in the absence of someone whose presence I have never known. And it seemed more real to me than all the presences. Perhaps this is what all human beings feel in the world, an exquisite loneliness, an absence unaccounted for. As for secrets, there are none. I have stopped believing that my life is littered with clues that I have failed to see. There will be no angel with news. It is I who am the skeleton in the cupboard. I have become the family secret. Shameful and dangerous like the shadow on an X-ray that speaks of death. A vessel of guilt, carrier of original sin, a child of Eve.

PART FOUR

THE BUS THAT took Irene Rivers – she had reverted to her maiden name – back to Granitefield was much the same as the one she had taken twenty years before. The same suitcases rattling overhead, the same nautical list as it negotiated corners. She could have sworn it was the same driver, but that couldn't be. The day was bright and silvery, reminding her of that day in another life when she had stopped to watch the waves dance in the autumn breeze and the *Queen Bea* drift into view. If she shut her eyes she could erase all that had happened in between, half a lifetime consumed in the blinking of an eye. The three-year jail sentence, reduced by six months for good behaviour. According to prison records she had been a model inmate, adapting well to institutional life. She did a stint in the prison kitchens. She seemed to have experience in this area and enjoyed the work. Almost, though the records did not state this, as if she had found her vocation. She received no visitors.

She was in high spirits as she walked up the driveway. She was well, her lungs were clear, and she was going home. It had all changed. It was no longer a sanatorium; the reign of the White Scourge had ended. It was now a home for the aged. Still a place of dread for some, but nobody held their breaths passing the gateway anymore. And all the people she had known were gone. Dr Clemens, Matron Biddulph, Gloria. She didn't presume them dead, however; Charlie Piper had cured her of that. The

221

isolation huts had all been torn down. New grass had been laid in their place with crescent beds of hectic daffodils. She climbed the front steps, gazing down proprietorially across the grounds to the lake, then turning, she stepped into the familiar hallway. She halted at the reception desk, no longer boxed in as it had been in Gloria's day to divide the healthy from the sick. A permed and soft-faced nurse sat behind it, a large ledger in front of her, a phone trilling at her elbow.

'Can I help you?'

Irene was dumbstruck. She didn't know why she was here except that it was the only place left to her.

The nurse took her in in one glance – a timid woman, slightly down-at-heel, wearing a well-worn coat, and a hat several years out of date.

'The kitchen job, is it?'

Irene nodded enthusiastically.

'Down the corridor, turn right, ask for Matron's office.'

'Oh yes,' Irene replied as the nurse silenced the phone. 'I know where that is.'

It's a live-in job, for which Irene is grateful, though there is a high turnover in the younger staff who cannot take the isolation. It suits Irene perfectly. In the afternoons, when the lull descends, she makes tea and sitting at the kitchen table she sifts through the mementos of a unique and poignantly short history. There is a strand of Pearl's hair, springy as a coil and glinting impishly when the light catches it. A single bright green mitten snapped from the string which once attached it to the child's coat, a painting she made of the house, a pleasing rectangle with puffs of charcoal from its chimney and the sun a bright yellow ball, a reader for beginners, *The Sleeping Beauty*, in the corners of whose pages are tiny teethmarks. And there are photographs of a plump-faced baby with a gummy smile and a mark on her chin.

'Is this your baby?' Clare, the kitchen maid, asked, coming across Irene alone with her treasures on one such afternoon. She is a gawky child, lanky and bravely awkward. She is the same age as Irene was when she came to Granitefield first; it makes her feel tender towards Clare. 'Yes, but she's a big girl now,' Irene told her, 'Fully grown.'

'And do you see her often?'

'Oh yes,' Irene tells her and for once it is not altogether a lie. She sees her every day, in fact, a child skipping ahead of her on a dusty street, arms spread wide greeting the future, a future Irene has relinquished. It gives her ease to know that Pearl has an existence, somewhere, even at a distance and with another mother. Better that than she were dead. The knowledge that she lives and breathes is enough to sustain Irene. Pearl is out in the world and as long as Irene lives, she is not lost but merely waiting to be found again.